FROM THIS DAY ON

When Nick arrives in a small Cornish village as doctor's locum, she's not expecting the opposition that she receives — just for being female! It seems that Doctor Roskelly, once left broken-hearted, now distrusts all women equally . . . But his Aunt Dolly, reputed to be a bit of a witch, intervenes, making Nick welcome. Gradually, the patients appreciate her — but can she ever hope to heal her own boss?

CHRISSIE LOVEDAY

---◆---

FROM THIS DAY ON

Complete and Unabridged

LINFORD
Leicester

First published in Great Britain in 2009

First Linford Edition
published 2010

British Library CIP Data

Loveday, Chrissie.
  From this day on. - -
  (Linford romance library)
  1. Women physicians- -Fiction.
  2. Substitute physicians- -Fiction.
  3. Cornwall (England: County)- -Fiction.
  4. Love stories. 5. Large type books.
  I. Title II. Series
  823.9′2–dc22

ISBN 978–1–44480–452–2

Published by
F. A. Thorpe (Publishing)
Anstey, Leicestershire

Set by Words & Graphics Ltd.
Anstey, Leicestershire
Printed and bound in Great Britain by
T. J. International Ltd., Padstow, Cornwall

This book is printed on acid-free paper

'I Don't Work Well
With Women'

Doctor Nick Quenby put her briefcase
down on the desk and feeling slightly
nervous, looked round the small consulting room. Bleak. Uninspiring. Bare
walls. Three chairs, including her own,
plus an elderly looking desk. An ancient
couch stood along one side and
venetian blinds covered the one small
window. At least she might add a few
pictures to brighten the place. She
opened the drawer of the desk. There
were prescription pads, a current copy
of Mimms, the drug bible and a
collection of envelopes and forms.
Looked straight forward enough, if
rather minimalist. There was a knock
on the door and it was pushed open.

'Oh, you're a woman.' The large, well
built man stared at her as if she was

some sort of alien.

'Well, yes, I'm certainly a woman. And could you be Doctor Roskelly?'

'They didn't say they were sending a woman. I don't work well with women,' he snapped, ignoring her question. 'Don't unpack. I doubt you'll be staying for long.'

'I'm not a man. And they didn't tell me that you were a misogynist, so we're equally ill-informed.' She bit her lip. She shouldn't have said that. Not a good beginning. She was angry at his words. He was boorish and impolite. 'I resent being condemned as a doctor just because I'm female. How dare you assume I'm no good without even seeing what I can do?'

He stared at her with the darkest eyes she had ever seen. They were almost black. Difficult to read any expression in them. He swept his hand over an unruly mop of black hair and almost gave a smile. More a grimace, she thought.

'I'm sorry,' he mumbled. 'I was just

shocked to see you. I was told you were young and fairly newly qualified but you were able to start right away. I had to take up the offer. I read Nick Quimble and assumed you were a man.'

'It's actually Quenby. Nick Quenby. Doctor Quenby, even. But where's the real Doctor Roskelly?' This brash younger man certainly wasn't what she was expecting.

'I am he. Quite real. One hundred percent Doctor Roskelly. Must get on.'

'Well, Doctor, perhaps we could try again. I'm Doctor Nick Quenby, how do you do?' She held out a hand to the man. He ignored it.

'Yes. Well, you'll have to do for now. I'll get in touch with the medical agency and see if they have any men on their books. Not the right sort of practice for a woman. Too many accidents and emergencies on both land and sea. This is Cornwall . . . not some city life. You'd be bored in no time. No nightclubs or theatres at this end of Cornwall.'

'Apart from the Minnack Theatre, of course. And there are even some nightclubs, I believe. I know the area well. I was born not far from here. My parents lived here for most of my childhood. They eventually moved to be near my married sister in Devon. So, all in all, I'm fully aware of the demands of living next to the sea.'

He frowned.

'We'll give it a trial. Couple of weeks should be enough to see if it's going to work out. Hobson's choice really. I couldn't get anyone else here for a long time and I'm desperate for help. The holiday season and all that.'

'Your previous partner left suddenly, I gather?'

'Had a serious motoring accident. Had to go into long term rehab. Poor man. Got to learn to walk again. I hope he'll be back one day but meantime, I had to get someone here to help out. Too much for one person to do.'

'I expect some of your female patients might be pleased to have a

4

woman to consult. It might even work out for us together.' He ignored her remark.

'Mrs Liddicoat will be in soon. She's the receptionist-cum-secretary and general dogsbody.'

'Another woman?' Nick couldn't help saying with a just a hint of sarcasm.

He made a humph noise and turned to leave the room. 'Patients will start arriving in about ten minutes. Ask Mrs Liddicoat for anything you need. She'll send their cards in with them.'

'I take it there isn't a computer?'

'No point. She'd never learn how to use it. I don't fancy spending all my spare time putting it right. Best get on.' He swept out of the room and shut the door noisily.

'That went well,' she muttered angrily. Who did he think he was? Madoc Roskelly could take a running jump as far as she was concerned. What on earth must his patients think of him? Especially the female patients.

He was the exact opposite of what

she had been expecting. The description of the small practice had led her to think she was moving to idyllic West Cornwall, the place where she'd been so happy as a child.

The Doctor Roskelly she'd thought she was to work with, must have been in his sixties. Her parents had known him and had asked to be remembered to him. This Madoc must be his son.

He could only be in his thirties but clearly had forgotten what it was like to be young. He was probably middle aged in his teens she thought with a slight giggle. What was his problem? He was actually rather good looking in a slightly unkempt way but nobody could ever live with a prejudiced chauvinist like that.

She heard the outer door open and wondered if Mrs Liddicoat had arrived.

Interested to see the woman who did manage to survive that man's temper, she opened the door and peered out. An elderly woman was hanging her coat on a peg on the back of the door.

'Oh my goodness, you're a woman,' she said. 'Emma Liddicoat,' she went on, holding out her hand.

'Nick Quenby. Pleased to meet you. And yes, as I said to Doctor Roskelly, I am indeed a woman.'

'Bet you didn't get much of a welcome. Sorry I wasn't here to stave off his lack of manners. He's a typical Leo. Can be very angry and positively ferocious at times but he's fiercely loyal once he gets to know you. Meanwhile . . . '

'It was a bit of a shock. Is he always this rude to women?'

'Pretty much. Was badly let down in his past. Never got over it and assumes all women are like that wife of his.'

'He's married?' she gasped in amazement. 'If he behaves this brusquely to everyone, how on earth do the patients cope?'

'Was married. As for his patients, surprisingly, most of them adore him. Especially the older ones. He's fine with them. He's not so good with children though. Can be a bit sharp at times.'

'Maybe that's where I can best help. I did a year in paediatrics during my training. Oh dear, I was so looking forward to working here. I hope I can make a go of it.'

'Despite our esteemed senior partner, you mean. You could be just what's needed around here. I'll put the kettle on and we'll try to re-start the day properly. Tea or coffee for you?'

'Coffee, please. Black and no sugar. Thanks for making me feel just a little bit welcome.'

* ★ ★

Nick went back into her consulting room and took out a few of her things from her briefcase. Her bright red desk tidy with a collection of writing implements and her own notebook (red again) and a little clock with a Pooh Bear face that waved as the seconds ticked by. The kids loved it and it made them relax. It wasn't much as yet to brighten the place, but it gave her a sense of something personal. A knock at the door and Mrs Liddicoat came in with a cup of coffee. She had several fat brown envelopes in her other hand containing patients' notes.

'Your first appointment might be a tricky one. It's Jed Younger from one of the farms. He can be a bit difficult. He's used to seeing Doctor Lavers, the one you're replacing and doesn't think anyone else is capable of treating his rheumatism.'

'That's all I need,' groaned Nick. 'What is it about the men around here?'

'Oh, it's not just the men. He wants to see his own doctor and won't accept that poor Doctor Lavers can't see anyone at present. If he ever does again. I'll send him to you in five minutes, shall I?'

'Fine. I'll look through his notes and see what treatment he's on.'

She saw that he'd been prescribed steroids at some time in the past but this had been discontinued. She saw a little note scribbled in pencil saying he failed to take pills regularly. She sighed. The steroids might have done him some good but he constantly failed to take them, it was hopeless and suddenly stopping them could be a disaster.

It was a case of anti-inflammatory drugs and perhaps organising some physiotherapy. She wondered how that worked around here. There must be somewhere to refer him. Something else she needed to find out. She felt very ill-prepared for the coming day.

She pulled her notebook towards her and wrote down her first question. *Where do I refer patients for physio?* She sighed. She should never have been placed in this situation without some guidance. Mr Younger came in. He stopped as he saw her.

'Where's the other one gone to?' he snapped.

'I'm sorry? I'm Doctor Quenby. Take a seat will you, Mr Younger.'

'I'n't right to keep changing people. Don't know where I am.'

'I've read your notes, Mr Younger. I think I may be able to offer you some different tablets. They'll help you, providing you take them regularly. It's mainly your hands, isn't it?'

'Pain me summat chronic they does.'

She looked at his twisted hands with their swollen joints. He could barely move his fingers at all and she smiled sympathetically. She gently took the gnarled hands and felt them as he tried to straighten the joints. She could see the pain in his pale watery eyes.

There was undoubtedly very little that could be done for the man. A farmer who had always worked outside in all weathers, he was clearly in the wrong job but she doubted he had any choice in the matter. She wrote out his prescription and handed it to him.

'Try these for a while. They might help. I'll see if there's anything else we can offer. We might be able to try some physiotherapy. I'll have to speak to Doctor Roskelly.'

They chatted for a few minutes

longer about his work and general lifestyle. He seriously needed to get some more help on his farm.

'You might be all right,' he muttered as he left. Nick raised her eyebrows. Was that a compliment? 'At least you listens to me.'

★ ★ ★

It was almost eleven o'clock by the time she had seen all her list of patients. One or two had actually welcomed her and seemed pleased to be able to discuss their problems with a sympathetic lady doctor.

'Survived then?' her boss asked as she emerged from her room. He gave her an almost grin . . . she thought it was the nearest she would get to a smile and felt grateful.

'Yes. Not bad. One or two things I shall need to ask you about. I'm keeping a list.'

'Did you manage to find somewhere to stay?' he asked unexpectedly.

'I'm not really sure. I stayed at the pub last night. I didn't arrive till six so it was a case of finding a bed for the night as soon as possible. Obviously I shall need somewhere more permanent. At least . . . ' she hesitated. 'At least till we know if I'm going to work here for longer than today.'

'About that. I'm sorry, Nicola. I was very tired when I met you. Been up all night with one of our older residents and I was shocked to see you. All the same, I shouldn't have taken it out on you. Been managing on my own for much too long.' His voice was a little gruff. He clearly found apologies difficult.

Nick looked at him. There were certainly lines around his eyes that suggested weariness.

'So, I take it I should find somewhere to stay for at least the rest of the week?'

'There's a little cottage along the lane. It belongs to an aunt of mine. She will probably let you have it for a reasonable rental. Under the circumstances, I don't suppose you'll even need to take out the normal rental agreement. She can treat it as a casual holiday type of let. I'll speak to her. You can go and take a look later. If it suits, well and good. Now, I should go and start my visiting list. Maybe you could spend a bit of time with Mrs Liddicoat. Find out how we work things.'

'Thanks. That would be good. She can probably answer most of my questions. By the way, it's Nick. I never respond to Nicola.'

'I might remember. Right. Must get on. See you later.'

She watched him stride round to the little car park. He was rather attractive in a way, as long as you didn't think about his bad temper. She wanted to discover more about him. Mrs Liddicoat . . . Emma . . . had hinted that his wife was, or had some sort of a problem. She would have to probe gently and see what else there was to know about this strange man.

'I've put out the biscuit tin for you to help yourself,' Emma told her as she handed Nick a mug of steaming coffee. 'Thought you might need a little energy boost.'

She smiled and sat down to enjoy a break. They spent some time talking through the way everything worked. It was very different to the places Nick had worked in before.

She had spent several months acting as locum in a group practice in a market town in the Midlands. There they had used a practice manager and had a whole team of secretarial staff so everything was organised to the minutest degree. She had also spent a longer period working in the A & E unit at the hospital where she had trained. Everything there had been high powered and dramatic, or so it seemed.

She just remembered being constantly exhausted and working impossible hours. She was looking forward to a more relaxed atmosphere where she could actually get to know her patients and be part of a community. That all looked a bit like a pipe dream now.

'Tell me about Doctor Roskelly. You said something about him being upset by his wife?'

'They're separated now. Didn't like living here, sharing her home with the practice. You realise Madoc lives here as well as working here? Anyway, she was a spoilt brat if you ask me. Wealthy parents. Private education. You know the sort of thing. Wanted to spend all her time partying and taking expensive holidays. Never destined to be a doctor's wife. Can't think how Madoc ever came to marry her.'

'And as a doctor, Madoc couldn't do all those things? Parties and such. So what did he see in her?'

'She's a very beautiful woman. They married young, well he was young for a doctor. She was several years younger than him. All done in rather a hurry. She was seen as quite a catch at the time.'

'So why did she want to marry him? If he hates women so much, what could have attracted her?'

'He can be extremely charming in the right circumstances. He's actually quite good looking, don't you think? Rugged hero type really. She, the wife, had an affair. Well, several in all honesty. I suspect it was the result of her problems actually. Madoc sort of turned in on himself and became what you see today. He'll come round. Especially if he sees you can cope with whatever comes along.'

'What problems?'

'I'm not one to gossip,' she lied. She gave a sheepish grin which belied her words. 'As I say, I expect he'll come round once he can see you're coping.'

'I'll do my best. So, what needs doing now?'

'I think you're clear till afternoon surgery. Four o'clock. I suggest you try and sort out somewhere more permanent to stay. I'll give you Madoc's aunt's number. In fact, why don't you go and call on Auntie Dolly right away?' She wrote the address on a slip of paper

17

and handed it to Nick. She gave her directions and sent her on her way.

* * *

It was a tiny village. Once relying on fishing as its main source of income, Gwillian was now a maze of holiday cottages and small shops supplying the needs of holidaymakers. Whitewashed walls and pots of bright red geraniums everywhere, it was the epitome of a quaint Cornish fishing village. The steep road led down to the tiny harbour where a few boats bobbed on the sea and heaps of lobster pots were piled alongside the stone jetty. It was more like a hobby, with tourist fishing as the main occupation rather than a serious commercial enterprise.

Nick found Auntie Dolly's cottage and knocked on the door. A tiny, grey haired lady answered. Nick realised she didn't even know her proper name.

'Miss er ... Mrs ... ' she floundered.

'Auntie Dolly. Everyone calls me Auntie Dolly. You must be the new doctor. How you gettin' on with that nephew of mine?'

'Yes, I am Nick Quenby, the new doctor. But how on earth did you know?'

'Word gets around. Heard you was a woman. Bet he doesn't like that. Not good with women, our Madoc.' Nick grinned wryly. She was clearly unused to this village mentality where everyone knew everyone's business.

'I expect we shall find a way to work together.' Bit hopeful, she mused.

'You'll be here about the cottage. It's small but good enough for one person. Got most of what you need. If it suits, you can move in right away. You'll not do with staying at that there public house. Not right for a woman on her own.'

'Well, yes, I had hoped to look at the cottage. If it isn't let for holidaymakers, of course.'

'No. I was keeping it by. Madoc said

he'd be having someone down to help him. Bachelor, or so he thought.' She gave a delighted chuckle. 'Bet you came as quite a shock. You'll do though. Reckon you can hold your own. Got that look about you.' Her dark eyes, so like Madoc's, twinkled. She fumbled in her apron pocket and produced a couple of keys on a ring. The label said *Myrtle Cottage*.

Nick had seen it as she'd walked down. It was delightful. Tiny, admittedly, but perfect for her. It overlooked the harbour and had a little stone seat outside, perfect for watching the world, such as it was, go by.

'Thank you. It looks gorgeous. I'll go and look right away and hopefully move in as soon as possible.'

'Oh, you'll like it all right. I can tell. And you and Madoc will become close. I know that as well.' She gave a cackle that made Nick stare. It was positively witch like. 'Yes, my dear. I can see what you're thinking. I do have powers. Known for it I am. If Madoc's

20

medicines don't work, they do come to me. I can usually provide them with something. If you need anything yourself . . . don't be shy. Might need one of my potions to snap that nephew of mine out of his bad habits.' Another cackle. Nick resisted the urge to giggle.

'Thank you Miss . . . Auntie Dolly. I'll go and look at the cottage right away.' She walked back along the little street, aware of a pair of sharp black eyes following her progress.

Nick Proves Her Worth

Myrtle Cottage was perfect. Assuming Auntie Dolly wasn't going to charge her too much rental, she would adore living there.

'Hello? Is that you in there, Doctor?'

Nick jumped. She ran down the stairs and saw Madoc standing in the little sitting room. Filling it, actually.

'Hi. Just thought it would be a good chance for me to look at your Aunt's place.'

'Will it suit?' he asked. He looked uncomfortable and awkward.

'It's gorgeous. Assuming I can afford the rent, it will be perfect.'

'Good. Rent won't be a problem.'

He was about to say something else when his mobile rang. 'Yes. How badly? Yes. Right. I'll be there right away. No. No problem. I've got to go. There's been an accident down by the harbour.'

'I'll come too. What sort of an accident?'

'A child. In the water. I'll manage. You carry on playing houses.'

'Don't be ridiculous. I'm coming too. I'll take the keys back later. I may be able to help. I'm good with children.'

'Really? Come on then.'

★ ★ ★

He set off at a frantic pace, jogging as he went down the hill. He was clearly very fit. Nick puffed along after him, making a mental note that she must take more exercise. A crowd had gathered around the water's edge and they could hear someone wailing as they got close.

'Quick, Doc. She's not breathing.'

'Save her, Doctor. She's my little girl. I barely took my eyes off her and she went under. That man pulled her out but she isn't breathing.' The mother of the child had tears pouring down her face. Madoc pushed her aside.

'Let me get to her. Get back everybody. Let me do my job. Has anyone called an ambulance?' The crowd moved back a little but everyone was still crowding in to see what was going on. Madoc looked up at Nick and there was helplessness in his eyes. The child was blue round the mouth and completely white faced. Nick knelt down beside her.

'You start chest compressions. I'll blow.' She placed her own mouth over the cold mouth of the child and gently blew in.

One, two, three. Madoc began compressions and counted. She blew again and he pumped some more. She felt the tiniest movement and nodded to Madoc. They turned her on to her side and she vomited violently and began to breath again. The crowd cheered and the mother fell upon her child and hugged her, scolding her as she did so for falling into the water. Madoc pulled out his mobile and called for an ambulance.

'On its way. Someone called earlier.'

'Sorry. They didn't tell me,' he snapped.

'Thank you. Thank you so much,' the grateful parents said over and over. Someone put a coat over the child. She was still icy cold. Nick lay down on the damp sand and held the dazed girl close to her, talking softly to her, comforting and warming her till the ambulance arrived.

The mother got into the vehicle with her daughter and the father went to get his car so he could follow behind.

'Should I go too?' asked Nick, not sure of the protocol.

'Please yourself, love,' the paramedic said. 'We can take it from here. I reckon she'll be fine with some oxygen and once the warming blanket has done its job.'

'OK, if you're sure. I have got surgery soon.'

'Looks like you did a good job, both of you.' He got into the driving seat and they were quickly clear of the scene.

The bystanders drifted back to their beach encampments and the harbour area soon looked back to normal.

'You'd better find some dry clothes,' Madoc suggested. 'You can hardly run a surgery with a soaking wet skirt all covered in sand. Are you all right? You did a good job there.'

'Why, thank you. We were a good team. Funny to think that twenty minutes, well thirty minutes ago, there was a virtually dead child lying there. Thank heavens we were close by. Lord, I wonder if I actually locked the cottage door. I don't remember. I'd better go back that way and check. I'm too late to move in there now. I'll have to go tomorrow.'

'I can help you after surgery. I'll buy you dinner too. To make up for my rudeness this morning. We can go back to the pub after we move you into the cottage.'

Nick stared at him in amazement. He sounded almost civil and it was most unexpected.

'It's very kind of you. But you don't have to. I can manage. I only brought a small amount of my stuff with me. Left it at my parents and planned to go and collect it at the weekend.'

'All the same. I owe you. The fact that you kept the child warm and talked to her so comfortingly, made me realise how lacking I am. I'd have left that to the parents. They were standing there like porridge. Come on. You're freezing.'

She saw that his hand was on her arm, an unconscious gesture that was beginning to have a strange effect on her. She stared at him and he took his hand away leaving a chilled patch where it had been.

What had Auntie Dolly said? You two will become close. Nonsense, of course. All the same, she wondered again what it might be like to be really close to this enigmatic man. He stared back at her again and a fleeting softening of his expression made her blush. It was as if he knew exactly what she had been

27

thinking. Perhaps he too had some sort of powers like his aunt.

'I should go and change. I'd better go back to the pub now or I'll be late for my surgery. Wouldn't do at all on my first day.'

'Shall I tell Auntie Dolly you'd like to take the cottage? You might as well hang on to the key and move in right away. I'll see you later. Don't worry if you're a bit late. I can see your first patients for you.'

'You're being uncharacteristically kind. Be careful or I might get used to it.'

'Nonsense. The sooner I get you settled, the sooner I can make use of your expertise. I'll see Auntie Dolly then. On my way back.' The corner of his mouth twitched. She didn't know whether to take him seriously or not. He was such an interesting man, she decided.

'Thanks. I'll be back at the surgery as soon as I've had a shower and I'll give my notice to the pub as well.'

'Book a table for this evening too. That way the old skinflint won't charge you rental for another night as you're late checking out.' He turned and began to walk briskly back up the hill. She crossed back to the pub and went inside. The landlord nodded to her.

'Good job there, Doc. Your first day as well.'

'Goodness, news travels fast in this place. I need to have a shower and get out of these wet things.'

'And you'll be giving me notice. Taking Auntie Dolly's place are you?'

She shook her head in disbelief. Did nothing stay private?

'That's right. Oh and Doctor Roskelly asked me to book a table for dinner this evening.'

'Crikey. That's a turn up. I wonder how you managed that one?'

'I'll be round after surgery to collect my luggage and pay you.'

'I'll just charge you for the one night. We usually ask our guests to sign out by noon but under the circumstances,

29

we'll let that pass. The room isn't needed tonight.'

'Well thanks. Kind of you.'

'Don't mention it. Anyone who can get a meal out of the Doc is something special.'

'You assume he's bringing me to eat here. It could be someone else.'

'Nah. Not him. He rarely comes in here. Doesn't drink and he's a vegetarian.' He said it as if it was some nasty disease.

'I must go. I'm due at the surgery in a few minutes.' She smelled food cooking as she went upstairs and her stomach rumbled. She hadn't got round to any lunch and had only eaten a couple of biscuits earlier that morning. Still, that would all change when she was settled into Myrtle Cottage.

So, Madoc was vegetarian was he? And he didn't drink, she thought as she showered. Maybe there was something to be said for a village grapevine after all. All sorts of useful information became available.

She quickly dressed and dumped her wet clothes into a plastic bag. She hadn't unpacked much last night so it would take a short while to clear the room later.

There were several people waiting in the little waiting-room. They looked up as she went in and some of them nudged each other. Emma Liddicoat was behind the desk, exactly where she was when Nick had left earlier.

'Hear you had an eventful afternoon,' she said.

'It was a bit. Is Doctor Roskelly seeing my patients?'

'Actually, no. He was called out to The Beeches. One of his ladies is ill. So, I'm sorry but you have a full house.' Nick nodded and went into her room. It was just as depressing as she remembered. She called in the first patient and apologised for being late.

Nick worked her way through the list of patients, feeling totally exhausted by the time she had finished at almost six o'clock. She was convinced that a number of them had invented minor ailments, simply to get a look at the new doctor. She went into the waiting-room, dreading seeing yet another person sitting on the line of chairs. Madoc was leaning over the desk, sorting through a stack of papers.

'I told Emma she could leave a little early. Any problems?' she asked.

'Not really.'

'I'll go and start my packing. Where shall I meet you?' Nick asked.

'Let's take your things to the cottage first, then we can relax. I'll call round to the cottage for you. I can help you in with your stuff. If we just dump it inside, we can go and eat right away and you can leave your car there so you can have a drink and not have to drive.'

'Oh, but I thought you didn't drink?'

'This village is impossible,' he snapped. 'I don't drink as it happens, but that's no reason why you shouldn't enjoy a glass of wine. Or whatever else it is you drink.'

'OK. Thanks. I'll go and pack and settle my bill and we'll meet at Myrtle Cottage. Shouldn't take me too long.'

* * *

Nick drove to her cottage and parked in the tiny area outside. It was a good job she had a small car or it would have overhung the road. She took her things inside and looked around again. It was delightful. A perfect place for one. She opened the fridge and found a carton of milk, a loaf of bread and some butter.

'How kind,' she murmured. In the cupboard there was a pot of homemade strawberry jam, her favourite kind, and a box of cereal, exactly the sort she always bought. Auntie Dolly must have been round and put in the supplies, using her strange powers to know exactly what would be needed for breakfast. She gave a grin . . . it was pure coincidence. As if anyone could really know such things. All the same . . .

There was a knock at the door.

'Come in,' she called, knowing it would be Madoc.

'Settling in all right?' he asked, sounding uncharacteristically cheerful.

'Just arrived. Your aunt seems to have put in some basic supplies. That's so kind of her. I haven't given a thought to shopping yet, so it's much appreciated. I'll pay her of course. Speaking of payment, I still don't know how much the rent is.'

'I'll deduct it from your pay. Very affordable anyway. Oh and don't offer to pay her for the shopping. She'll be offended. It's what people do around here. Now, if you're ready to eat? Or do you want help carrying things in?'

'I've already brought my bags in. I was just going to put the wet clothes in the washer and then I certainly am ready to eat. Just smelling the food at the pub made me realise how hungry I am.'

★ ★ ★

They strolled down the little lane looking almost companionable to the outside world. The conversation was slightly strained however and Nick wondered if it could ever be any different. Madoc opened the door politely and touched her elbow as she passed him. She felt a slight jolt and jumped slightly. He pulled his hand back and looked away, embarrassed.

'Sorry,' he mumbled.

'It's nothing,' she stammered back. This was ridiculous. They were both stupidly tense. He couldn't cope with women and she was behaving like a teenage idiot, jumping at the slightest touch. How on earth would they be able to work together unless they both sorted themselves out.

'I've put you at the table in the corner,' the landlord told them. 'Thought you might prefer that to the window seat where everyone can see you.'

'We've nothing to hide. I expect the entire village knows we're sharing a table. We'll sit by the window. Doctor

Quimble might like to look at the sea.'

'Quenby,' Nick snapped irritably. 'And yes, the sea view will be excellent.' At least she might have something other than this bad tempered man to look at. The landlord walked away with a grin on his face.

A young girl arrived with menus.

'There're specials on the board as well,' she told them. 'Can I get you something to drink while you're deciding?'

'Mineral water. Ice. No lemon,' Madoc snapped.

'I'll have the same,' Nick decided.

'You're welcome to have wine,' he suggested.

'I'll have wine with my meal, when I've decided what I want to eat.'

It was an extensive menu for so small a place. She was pleasantly surprised, having settled for just a sandwich the previous evening when she arrived. She glanced at the board and was torn between one of the steaks she'd heard about and the fresh fish dishes. She opted for the latter, thinking she could eat steak anywhere but freshly caught lemon sole was much rarer. Madoc also chose fish.

'Oh, you're not a strict vegan or anything,' she said.

'I eat fish as it's so healthy and provides good protein. I just avoid meat. It doesn't agree with me.'

'And alcohol? You don't like it or is there some other reason?'

He glared at her and immediately she wished she could have withdrawn the words. She was being much too nosy and personal. 'I'm so sorry. I shouldn't have asked that. Nothing to do with me.'

'No, it isn't. Look I suggest we keep off the personal and talk about the practice. Safer that way. This was only your first day. How do you feel it went?'

'All right, I suppose. I have to get to grips with the various protocols of referring people for treatment and so on and see your list of exactly which prescription medicines are allowed.'

The food arrived and the conversation continued on safe, work related topics.

'They don't seem exactly friendly,' the young waitress told the chef. 'Just talking shop all the time. Hoped it might have made old grump there a bit more human.'

Nick Is Proving Popular

The two doctors left the pub around nine o'clock and walked up the hill to the cottage. 'Thank you very much for a lovely meal. If that's the standard of cooking, I might become a regular customer there. I'm not much of a cook myself. My mother's a wonderful cook so I never needed to learn. Would you like a coffee?'

'Not this late, thank you. Besides, it wouldn't do for me to be seen leaving your place any later than this.'

'My goodness, the gossips certainly do ensure that everything's kept under tight control here. Nobody would dare step out of line.'

'We have a position to maintain in the village and around. As you say, the gossips find plenty to talk about without us giving them extra fuel. I'll see you in the morning. I suggest you leave your car here. It's not far and parking is a bit limited at my place. You won't need your car for visits yet. I'll do the home visits for a few days until you get to know the area.'

'Fine. I'll see you in the morning. And thank you again for the meal.'

He nodded, lightly touched her arm and strode off. It was just beginning to get dark and Nick looked down at the little harbour. Light reflections twinkled in the water and a new moon was rising. 'Picturesque or what?' she muttered as she went inside.

Luxuriating in her own surroundings for the first time in ages, she sat on the comfy sofa and stretched out her legs. If she had some chocolate, she would have made a cup. Perhaps Auntie Dolly's witchcraft has spirited some into the cupboard. She went to look, but no such luck. She could have a coffee but that might stop her sleeping. She switched on the little television and watched the news and then yawned.

She needed an early night. It had been quite a day.

*   *   *

She was awoken at six o'clock by the telephone. There was one next to her bed and the other downstairs in the kitchen. Unfamiliar with her new room, she almost fell out of bed and went to the door, then realised it was ringing behind her. Who on earth could it be at this ungodly hour?

'Nicola? It's Madoc Roskelly. Sorry to call so early but there's an emergency at The Beeches. One of my patients, a Mrs Clements has had a heart attack. I need to be there.'

'Do you want me to come?'

'Of course not,' he almost snapped. 'No, I've just had a call from Alice Penweather, our local midwife. She's got a difficult home birth and needs a doctor right away. If you go to that one, I'll see to Mrs Clements.'

'It's Windridge Farm. Out on the

41

Penzance Road and off to the left.' He gave her a phone number in case she got lost. 'I assume you have a local map. It's Symms Lane.' There was someone calling in the background. 'Yes. I'm just on my way, OK, Nicola. Get yourself there as soon as you can.'

He put the phone down and she rushed to find some clothes. Map. There must be a map somewhere. She had a large-scale map in the car and hoped that would do. Car keys. Medical bag. She grabbed everything and rushed to the door. She hadn't even brushed her teeth or combed her hair but she doubted either mother or baby would care about that.

She drove out towards Penzance, having seen various possible roads on the map. She had vague recollections of the area and just hoped she would find it easily.

'Symms Lane, Symms Lane,' she muttered. The roads were deserted and the sun was shining. If she had more time, she would be enjoying her early drive but the sense of urgency was pushing her on. She ought to get satellite navigation, she decided. Or at least a decent map.

She spotted the turning just too late and did a wide u-turn in the road. A milk lorry came along and hooted at her. She waved apologetically and drove down the lane. She saw the farm's sign and turned in thankfully. It was almost six-thirty.

She walked into the kitchen, calling out as she did so. An anxious man was standing at the bottom of the stairs, looking a bit helpless.

'Hi, I'm Doctor Quenby. Nick.'

'Alan Symms. Go straight up, Doc. They'll be pleased to see you, especially as you're a woman. Some problem. If it was a sheep in trouble, I guess I'd know exactly what to do. Bit different when it's your own wife.' Nick grinned as she went upstairs. Typical farmer's remark.

The midwife was working on her patient.

'Nick Quenby,' she introduced herself briefly. 'What's the problem?'

'We seem to be almost there actually. I was concerned that the second stage was taking too long and she was too far along to move her to the hospital. I wasn't happy with her progress and needed some extra help, just in case.'

'OK, gently does it at first,' Alice calmed her patient.

'I'll let you carry on, Alice. I'm here to support you. You're both doing a splendid job.'

Then it was soon all over. 'Another girl,' Alice told the panting mother. The baby yelled and everyone breathed a sigh of relief.

'She's lovely,' Nick said, her voice emotional. However many births one saw, each one was so special. 'I'll hold her shall I?' Alice completed severing the cord and they laid the baby on her mother's chest.

'Oh, Darling, well done,' the husband said, flinging his arms round his wife. 'Well done.'

'Hello baby,' Mary murmured.

'I'm sorry we didn't manage a boy,' Mary whispered to her husband.

'Don't be silly. I'm just pleased we have a healthy baby. What shall we call her?'

'I don't know. I never got beyond boys' names, hoping that might make it a boy.'

'I'd like a Cornish name. How about Tamzin?'

'That's nice,' said Nick. 'What are the others called?'

'Polly and Sarah. They're both still asleep, despite all the noise. Look, shouldn't I be making tea or something? And I have to get out to do the milking. I'm terribly late and I'm on my own at present.' Alan looked worried.

'OK. All done. We'll see to the other girls. You go and sort your cows,' Nick offered impulsively. She bit her lip. She would be needed at the surgery in half an hour and if Madoc was delayed on his call, there would be a real problem.

'Thanks so much,' Alan said, rushing

off. He almost fell over the two little girls, clad in pink frilly pyjamas, who were standing outside the bedroom door.

'We heard noises,' said the older one. 'Is it our new baby come?'

'Yes,' their dad said. 'Is it OK if they come and meet Tamzin?' he asked, rushing down the stairs.

'Of course,' Alice said quickly covering her patient and handing the baby over, wrapped in a towel. Nick ushered them into the room and they clustered round their mother, looking at the tiny new baby in awe.

'Is she a sister?' Polly asked.

'Yes and she's going to be Tamzin, we think. Do you like that name?' Mary asked.

'It's all right. She's very ugly and wrinkly, isn't she? All scrunched up.' Nick smiled. Not what a new mother wants to hear at all, she thought.

'Why don't you two show me where to make some tea for your mum? And we can get you dressed and ready to help. Is there someone coming to stay with you?' she asked hopefully.

'My mum's on her way down but she won't be here till later today,' Mary murmured weakly. Alice could see she was completely exhausted and needed a good rest.

'You relax. I'll sort out little Tamzin and Nick will see to the girls for a while. Then we'll see what we can do to get some help for you.' Alice took the baby and left Mary to rest. 'Can you manage this?' she asked Nick.

'Sure. Well no, not really. I have morning surgery in about fifteen minutes. Doctor Roskelly was called out on another emergency. I'll give the surgery a call and see what's going on.'

She ushered the two little girls down the stairs and went into the warm kitchen. She put the kettle on the large range and grabbed bowls and cereal from the cupboard next to it. 'Can you put some out for yourself and Sarah?' she asked Polly.

'Yes I can. But she's got to eat it. She

isn't always a good girl with cereal, are you Sarah?'

'No,' said the small girl, banging her spoon into the empty bowl.

'She'll have to show Tamzin what to do from now on, won't she? We don't want the new baby to see anyone being naughty, do we?' Two little faces, almost identical in their blonde colouring, smiling up at her with their heads nodding in tandem. Good as gold, they began to eat cereal. Nick took out her phone and dialled the surgery.

'Mrs Liddicoat? Emma. It's Nick. I'm stuck out at Windridge Farm for a while. I'm afraid I'm going to be late for surgery. Is Doctor Roskelly back yet?'

'I'm afraid not. He's still at the nursing home.'

'Oh dear. We have a new baby, a busy farmer and two little girls to be looked after. I'll see if Alice can do anything. Sorry. Please apologise to my patients and say I'll be there as soon as I can.'

'Fine. Any idea when it will be?'

'I'll call you back in a few minutes.'

Nick dashed upstairs and saw that Alice had finished washing the baby and was lying her in the little crib. 'I need a word,' she hissed. 'I have to go to surgery. Doctor Roskelly is still out on a call and I have patients waiting. I'm really sorry but I'll have to leave you. Is there anyone you can call till Granny arrives?'

'One of those mornings that's going to last all day, I guess. I'll stay for a while and get them sorted. I've been up all night so what's a few hours more. I'm off for the rest of the day. Perhaps Alan can come back in once milking's over and his stock are fed. Go on. I'll be down in a mo. Did you manage to sort some tea? I think Mary could do with a cup.'

★ ★ ★

By the time she could get back, she was almost an hour late for her patients. Feeling desperately embarrassed, she went into the waiting room to face the grumpy crowd.

'I'm so sorry. I was delayed at an emergency.'

'Mrs Symms' baby? We heard she'd started. Bet it's another girl.' The elderly lady was smiling and nodding expectantly.

'Well yes,' Nick agreed. It was hardly confidential and they'd all know within two minutes anyhow, knowing this place. 'Mother and baby doing well. A girl.'

'I knew it. Doubt they'd know what to do if a boy came along,' she laughed, nudging her neighbour.

'Right, well I'll just collect the notes and see whoever is first in a couple of minutes.' She went into her consulting room, followed by Emma, who carried a bundle of the brown envelopes.

'I've made you a coffee and put a biscuit with it. I don't suppose you managed any breakfast so I ordered a bacon roll to be sent in for when you finish.'

'You're a miracle,' Nick said grate-fully.

★ ★ ★

It was almost eleven o'clock by the time she had finished seeing the collection of people waiting for her. She felt totally exhausted as wearily, she went into the reception area. Emma was waiting with another coffee and the most wonderful smelling bacon roll. Madoc was stand-ing by the desk, already munching his belated breakfast, a hot cheese toastie.

'Nicola, I'm so sorry I didn't get here soon enough to help you. You look worn out. Sit down and eat your roll and relax for a few minutes.' Nick smiled up at him and took the food.

It was possibly the best thing she had ever tasted, she decided. 'Look, I'm sorry to land you with that,' Madoc continued in a kindly voice that sounded almost out of place from the big man.

'It's what I'm here for,' she replied.

'How was your patient?'

He looked away and bit his lips together.

'Not so good. I'm afraid we lost her. I did what I could but it was too late.'

'I'm sorry,' Nick said somewhat inadequately, she felt. She was seeing a more tender side of Madoc for the first time. He frowned and nodded.

'She was a great character. I used to enjoy her company and I'll miss her.'

'Life and death all in one morning,' Nick remarked. 'We meet it all don't we?'

'All part of the job. I gather you did a good job with Mrs Symms. Thank you. Now, you should go home and relax for a bit. I've got a few house calls and then I'll grab some lunch. Make sure you get some proper food to eat too, won't you?'

'I'll have to find some shops and stock up. Apart from what Auntie Dolly left for me, there's nothing edible in the place. Maybe I could cook supper for you? In return for you taking me out last night.'

'Well, if you're sure. That would be nice. We need to get to know each other better if we're going to be working together.'

'Does that mean I've passed my first test.'

'Certainly. I think things might just work out, despite . . . '

' . . . Me being a female?'

'I wasn't going to say that.' He gave a sheepish grin and once more, touched her arm as he left. For someone claiming to dislike women, he was quite demonstrative.

Nick smiled and winked at Emma, who was listening to the exchanges with great interest. She fingered the place on her arm where Madoc had touched her. She sensed that there was some strange chemistry between them, despite all her initial doubts. Auntie Dolly may have known something after all. Perhaps one day they might well become close.

An Uneasy Truce Arises

Back in her little cottage, Nick collapsed into the comfy armchair. Within seconds, she had drifted off to sleep. An hour later she awoke with a start, wondering where she was and why she had a crick in her neck. She glanced around the room and groaned at the washing still draped everywhere. She needed to get herself organised. She had barely even explored the place properly and hadn't found an ironing board or looked at the pots and pans.

She spent a while searching through cupboards and went outside the back door to the little outhouse which held an assortment of garden tools and chairs, a clothes line and pegs. That was something at least, she thought. A place to dry clothes was essential.

She glanced at her watch. She had a couple of hours before surgery and she needed to organise something for supper. She almost regretted her impulsive invitation to Madoc but it was too late. The menu would depend on what was available in the village.

She tidied the washing, unpacked the rest of her clothes and went off to the shops. Everyone smiled and nodded to her as she progressed up the street and would have stopped for a gossip if she had allowed herself to slow down at all. Everyone knew exactly who she was and were inevitably curious to meet the new G.P.

She stopped to look in the butcher's window, just to see what sort of things he stocked. No use for this evening, she thought. It all looked delightfully fresh and wholesome and she would enjoy being a customer there from time to time. She moved along to the vegetable shop, which also stocked a small range of packed goods and frozen food. She pushed open the door. The comfy looking, middle aged woman greeted her.

'Hello Doctor. Welcome to Gwillian. I'd heard you'd moved in and hoped you'd be visiting us soon. Now I don't know your taste in fruit and veg but I'd recommend our organic veggie boxes. They come in two sizes. You'd be wanting the smaller one. Packed by the Younger family they are. Sideline for the younger family . . . oh dear, that sounds confusing, doesn't it? I mean the son, Jed's son that is. He and his wife do the boxes weekly. Shall I put you down for one?' Nick stared, slightly overwhelmed by the torrent of words that greeted her.

'I . . . I suppose so. Yes please. It would be nice. I'm not quite sure of my plans just yet, though. Actually, it might be worth my waiting for just a little while. I can always buy what I need from you, can't I?'

'Oh yes, of course. Does that mean you don't like the thought of living here? Haven't you been given a proper welcome? Dear me, that isn't right. Now, why don't you pop round this evening and have a drink with me and my husband? Got a fresh batch of elderflower champagne just ready.'

'That's very kind of you but I'm busy this evening. And I've been welcomed here very nicely, thank you.'

'You don't have to take too much notice of Doctor Roskelly. He's a pussycat, really.' Discomforted, Nick stared at the woman. Was there nothing that could be kept private in this village?

'I need some vegetables for this evening. I'm cooking supper for my colleague. We have a lot to discuss.'

'Course you do, dear. Now I happen to know he's partial to aubergine and you can make a nice stuffing with a few onions and tomatoes. Oh and you'll need some rice to go with it.' She was packing assorted items into paper bags as she was talking, weighing them and jotting down prices on another brown paper bag. Nick felt as if she had gone back in time to when she used to go shopping with her gran. 'Right now, what are you planning for pudding? We've got some lovely strawberries and the local clotted cream to go with them. What do you think?'

'Thanks. That will do fine.' Her mind was in a whirl. 'Thanks, Mrs Fletcher. I assume it is Mrs Fletcher?' The sign outside read Fletcher's Fruit and Flowers.

'Maggie, Doctor. It's Maggie. No ceremony here.' She looked expectantly at Nick for the compliment to be returned.

'I'm Nick Quenby.'

'Oh, no wonder he thought you were a man. Hope you managed to keep on good terms with him. Like I say, he's a pussycat really. Now, if that's everything, that comes to five pounds and four pence. Forget the pence. Call it a welcome to the village.'

Nick stifled a grin. Four pence, eh? Still, the cost of the shopping was very small compared to the prices she was used to paying. 'Now, then, shall I tuck it all into a box for you? Unless you've got your own bag?'

'Sorry no. I haven't brought one. A box would be great, thanks.'

'I could get our Tommy to drop it round later if it helps?'

'I can manage, thanks. Goodbye for now.'

'Goodbye, Nick. Look forward to serving you in the future. Bye.'

She finally escaped and climbed back up the hill to her cottage, almost wishing 'our Tommy' had been pressed into service. She just hoped she could manage to produce a decent meal on the goods she had bought. There was nothing else in the fridge or cupboard so it would have to do. Maybe she needed to find a larger supermarket somewhere and stock up on basics. Tomorrow, she decided.

She wandered out of the back door and into the tiny garden. There were several areas where plants were growing and as she explored she recognised several different herbs. That would add flavour to the meal. She gave a little smile. It was to be expected that Auntie Dolly's house would have herbs growing in the garden. Ready for her various potions, no doubt.

Nick put away the shopping, wondering how one made stuffed aubergine. Couldn't be so very difficult she assumed. She wasn't much of a cook and relied on simple foods that could be grilled or put in a roasting tin to cook in the oven.

She glanced round the kitchen and saw a couple of books on a shelf. Cookery books she realised with pleasure. One looked rather elderly and had various recipes handwritten at the back. Amazingly, one was for stuffed aubergines. Auntie Dolly's work? She glanced through the list of ingredients, garlic. She had no garlic. She might need to go back to Maggie's to buy some. There was a knock at the door and a teenage boy stood there, clutching a brown paper bag.

''Scuse me, Doctor. My mam thought you might need this.' He held out the bag, containing garlic.

'I can't believe it,' she murmured. 'I was just thinking about garlic and how I didn't have any. I assume you're Tommy? Thank you so much.'

'S' alright. Mam said Auntie Dolly's recipe needed garlic so she sent it up.'

'Amazing. Seems everyone in this village has special powers. Did she say how much I owe? I'll settle up next time I'm in the shop.'

'It's OK. On the house. Bye then.' He turned and trotted back down the hill. This place was going to take a bit of getting used to.

* * *

Nick made herself a sandwich and some tea and went back to the surgery. Emily was sitting at an old manual typewriter, addressing envelopes.

'I really can't believe you haven't got a computer here. It makes everything so slow. How on earth do you keep up with things?'

'Madoc has one in his room. He deals with everything that comes in with that email thingy and I do all the records and mailing. It seems to work. I could never manage one of those evil things.'

'Oh, Emily, you are funny. It isn't so difficult you know and typing is very much easier on the hands and wrists than that old thing.'

'Madoc seems to think I'd break it too easily. I haven't bothered really. But, maybe we can discuss it at the practice meeting at the end of the week, if you think it may be a good idea. We meet on Fridays over lunch, in case he hasn't told you.'

Patients were beginning to arrive for surgery so the conversation ended there and she went into her gloomy little room and sorted out her notes. There seemed to be more women coming to see her than men and she smiled to herself. So much for equality.

Some of their ailments were very minor and she saw it still as an excuse to meet the new doctor. There was a fairly wide catchment area for the practice with people coming into the village from several of the other smaller villages around. She was unfamiliar with the area and would need to learn her way around. At last the final patient had been seen and Nick emerged to find Madoc once more sitting at Emily's desk.

'Emily gone home?' she asked.

'Yes. I don't like her working too late when surgery overruns. Can't be helped. Not a criticism of you. I think everyone's curious to see you. Oh, leave the patients' notes loose in the filing cabinet. Emily will put them away in the morning. Any problems this evening?'

'No. As you say, mild symptoms and major curiosity mostly. I'll get off now and start on supper. Seven-thirty all right for you?'

'Perfect thanks. Can I bring anything?'

'Not really, thanks. Oh, unless there's

anything special you like to drink. I never thought of that and only have water or water to offer.'

'I'll bring something. I can get some wine if you'd like it?'

'No need. I'm happy not to drink alcohol. See you later than.'

She walked the few yards back to her cottage. Her cottage. That sounded good. She set about following Auntie Dolly's recipe and soon the air was filled with the savoury smell of onions and garlic cooking.

She hummed as she worked and decided she must learn to cook properly. It couldn't be so difficult. Her mum, bless her, had always sent her out of the kitchen when she was a child, insisting she needed to do her homework or go and read something useful. It was a kind thought but had left her with few skills in the home.

She picked some herbs, unsure of which were which but they smelled good, so she chopped them up and added them to the mixture. Bake in a slow oven for one hour she read. It was ten minutes past seven. Without a pre-dinner drink, it was going to be a long wait. She didn't even have a starter or nibbles to slow things down. It was all going to be a disaster.

She washed the strawberries and put them into two dishes and left them on one side. They could always start with the dessert, she mused. Or toast. That was the only other thing she could make. Supermarket tomorrow, definitely, she decided.

Promptly at half-past seven. Madoc arrived, clutching a bottle of sparkling apple juice and a pack of savoury cheese twists. The man was a genius, she decided.

'Come in. Welcome. Thank you,' she added as he handed over his gifts. 'Supper will be a little while but we can have a drink and your cheese savouries.' He looked awkward in the little room, filling it with his large frame. 'Please, do sit down. I'll get some glasses and a plate.' She checked in the oven. It smelt good but when she prodded the aubergines, they were still very hard. She may need to use the microwave but that meant taking everything out of the roasting tin and she could end up with a disaster.

'You're not making stuffed aubergines are you?' Madoc asked.

'Well, yes. Maggie Fletcher said it was one of your favourites. I also happened to find a recipe in one of Auntie Dolly's books. I slightly misestimated the timing though. I'm afraid it will take a while yet.'

'Not to worry. We need to discuss various aspects of the practice anyway. Let's do that first, while we enjoy the drinks.'

After half an hour, Nick felt encouraged by everything he was saying. It seemed she wasn't to be sent away after the first week and he seemed to be accepting that she was a good doctor. They talked through the routine and how the home visits and surgeries were to be shared. She even broached the subject of installing a computer in the reception area.

'It would be so much quicker for Emily to type out letters and envelopes. And all the patient-records could be kept easily available. We could have a network system in both consulting rooms too.' Madoc stared at her. She drew breath to speak again but thought better of it.

'Nicola. I know you came from a large city practice before you arrived here. This is Cornwall. This is a very small practice. Emily would freak out if I suggested a computer.'

'No she wouldn't. I spoke about it this afternoon. She sounded quite enthusiastic, in fact.' He glared at her.

'All the same. I can't afford to spend money installing complicated systems. It was good enough for my father and if Doctor Lavers manages to regain his health and return here, he'd be lost.'

'Do you think he will ever return?'

'I hope so. I don't count on it, but I'd hate him to feel he was being cut out of it in any way. Now, how do you think those aubergines are doing?' She gave a shrug and went to look.

'Tell me some more about your elderly patients at the Beeches. How many are there living there?'

He talked as they ate. The food was surprisingly good and Nick felt pleased with herself. He was appreciative and seemed to relax. She longed to ask him about his private life but knew it was the wrong thing to do. He seemed enthusiastic about his work and clearly loved living in Cornwall.

'How are you going to cope with living in this isolated area?' he asked. 'Don't you miss the city life?'

'Not really. As I said, I spent most of my youth around here. I loved surfing and sailing and well, most water sports.'

'Now, I should be going. As usual, it's an early start for both of us and we didn't exactly have a lie-in this morning. I'll help you with the dishes and then be on my way,' he said.

'No need. There aren't many and I

can always leave things to soak if necessary.' He glared at her.

'Leave them to soak? I'm surprised at you. Poor hygiene. I insist on helping you.'

'I don't need your help,' she snapped. 'I can manage perfectly well and my hygiene standards are perfectly fine thank you.'

'Very well. Thank you for a nice meal. See you in the morning.'

He went out into the twilight and she watched him walk up the hill. What a cheek, she thought. All the same, she washed everything and dried it carefully before putting it away in the cupboards.

Her weariness afterwards suddenly hit her. It had been a very long day and she felt exhausted. Another early night, she decided. Somehow, life was going to be more demanding here and the idea of a social whirl was very far from her prospects. Perhaps this had been an unusual day but she doubted it.

★ ★ ★

Nick looked around the waiting-room the following morning. She had arrived slightly early for morning surgery, planning to see if there were some improvements that could be made. It was a bare room, nothing much to interest anyone waiting for appointments.

There should be leaflets around and things to inform patients. Some pictures on the wall would also brighten things up. Perhaps she might get some of her own photographs printed and framed. She was a keen amateur and had some lovely shots of Cornish cliffs and beaches.

She would mention it to Madoc, perhaps at the practice meeting. He came through from his kitchen, at the back of the waiting-room.

'Oh, good morning. I didn't hear you come in.'

'Perhaps we should have some sort of bell or buzzer when anyone comes in. It might be safer to know when anyone is here.'

'This is Cornwall not some town up-country. I can trust everyone in the village.'

'But you don't know everyone. Especially with so many visitors around. And I was thinking, we should put out some leaflets. Informative leaflets about various conditions. There are plenty around produced by suppliers and charities.'

'Not sure why. The ones who really need them will never read them. They'll just litter the village.'

'You have a low opinion of your patients.'

'Reality, my dear Nicola. Reality. Now, I must check on my list for this morning. Are you happy to do some home visits today?'

'Of course. I could do with a map though. I haven't got a detailed one for the area.'

'I'm sure Emma has something tucked away. She'll help you. Oh, thank you again for last evening.'

'My pleasure,' she murmured as the

phone rang. 'Sounds as though we're in business. Shall I get it?'

'No. Leave it for the machine. They know perfectly well that we don't begin taking calls until eight-thirty. They just hope to steal a march and get in first. Emma will sort it out when she gets here. She won't be long.'

'Right. Well . . . right.' Not quite knowing what else to say, she went into her consulting room and tidied her already tidy desk. The phone rang again but not wanting to upset Madoc for the day, she left it to Emma. She began making some notes, partly in preparation for the promised meeting. She heard a noise in the waiting room and she went to see what was happening. Someone was calling. A delivery man was standing by the desk, clutching a basket of flowers.

'Can I help?'

'You shouldn't leave this place unattended. I could have made off with all manner of stuff. Drugs and all, I shouldn't wonder.'

'Yes; well we're thinking of installing a warning bell for when the door opens.'

'That'd drive anyone mad. Ring, ring, ring every two minutes.'

'Can I help you?'

'You know the lady doctor here? I never heard there was a lady doctor round here, but the bloke on the phone assured me there was one.'

'I'm Doctor Quenby. I'm a female and I work here. Am I the one you're looking for?'

'S'pose you must be. These are for you.' He handed her the basket and she stared. 'Bye then.' She looked for a card. Who on earth could be sending her flowers? She tore open the miniature envelope.

Thank you for all your help yesterday. The Symms family, especially Tamzin.

'Oh how lovely but I scarcely did anything.' But nobody was listening. Emma came in.

'Good morning. My word, someone's

popular. How nice.'

'It's the Symms family. I scarcely did anything. It was all Alice, the midwife's work.'

'They'll have sent some flowers to her too, no worries. It's how people are round here.'

Nick carried the basket into her room and set it down on the side table. Immediately, the room looked brighter, more cheerful and welcoming. She must do something more permanent with it. Her picture would make a start. It was too much to expect Madoc to allow it to be re-decorated. Light coloured paint instead of the tired, elderly floral wallpaper would make a huge difference.

Maybe she could give it a coat of paint herself, over a weekend. Something else to ask at the meeting. There was a knock at her door and Emma came in clutching the patient notes.

She worked through her list and treated, reassured and sometimes, just talked things through with her patients.

She was gasping for a coffee when she finally cleared her list. Emma had it ready and waiting.

'I put the kettle on when your last one went in. Black isn't it? Or do you want a drop of milk in it?'

'Black's fine, thanks. If you've got time, I'd be grateful if you could point out on a map where these home visits are. I don't know this area all that well.'

'I'd be delighted. Just hang on while I take Madoc his coffee. He seems a bit stuck with his patient.'

The waiting-room door opened and an elderly woman came in. She managed the door with the aid of her two walking sticks and sat down heavily on the chair nearest Madoc's surgery.

'Can I help?' Nick offered.

'What's happened to Emily Liddicoat? You the new receptionist?'

'No, I'm Doctor Quenby. I'm helping Doctor Roskelly while Doctor Laver recovers.'

'You left school, have you?' the woman asked with a chortle.

'Of course. I'm a fully qualified doctor, nearly as old as Doctor Roskelly.'

The woman made a sort of grunt of disapproval.

'Wonderful man he is, that Madoc Roskelly. Don't get many like him to the pound. Always patient. Always wants to listen.'

'Of course. He's with a patient at the moment. I don't suppose he'll be long. I take it you have an appointment?'

'Don't hold with appointments. I comes along when I needs to. He always sees me.'

Emma came out of Madoc's room.

'Oh, Mrs Christopher. I didn't realise you were coming in today. I'll see if Doctor is able to see you.'

'I can see her if you like.'

'Don't want no schoolgirl seeing me thank you very much. I want my own doctor. He always knows what's wrong with me. Always knows what medicine I need. Lovely man he is. Kind and patient.'

Emma had gone into Madoc's room and told him Mrs Christopher was waiting. An elderly man with silver hair came out, shaking hands and almost bowing to Madoc as he left. He went outside and touched the place where his hat might have been as he saw Mrs Christopher waiting.

'I'm sorry to keep you waiting,' he said politely. 'I'm afraid I've overrun my time. Haven't seen you for a while ma'am.'

'No I haven't been up here for a while. I've been a bit poorly. But, it's a nice sunny morning, so I thought I'd come up and see the Doc.' The pair chatted for a few moments and Nick was fascinated by the conversation and the accents of the two. It was the old joke personified. Been too ill to come and see the doctor but I'm here now I'm feeling better.

A Happy Routine
For Nick

The next couple of days were busy and very satisfying to Nick. She felt she was at last working somewhere that she could enjoy and do a good job. She had taken on most of the local children as they came to visit the surgery and their parents were delighted to find someone who had both skill and patience to deal with the younger ones.

Madoc was also relieved to find that he no longer needed to face the daily rounds of children, whom he believed were sent to try him. Nick was able to manage the Gwillian surgery while Madoc worked the occasional surgery opening hours at other villages. It was a service they were again, able to provide for the elderly patients who were unable to travel to Gwillian. By Friday lunchtime, they had both cleared their lists and Emma had organised a sandwich lunch for them all as they had the promised meeting.

They sat round Madoc's kitchen table, the outside door to the waiting-room firmly locked. All the villagers knew of the regular Friday meeting and that it was pointless to try to see anyone for the precious hour. Holidaymakers were less informed and often rang the bell outside, defying the notice that clearly stated there was nobody available over the lunch period. Nick had her notepad ready to write down anything that she needed to know and also had her own suggestions listed. She planned to keep quiet at first, know that it was hardly her place to make comment, especially as she was such a temporary addition.

It was fairly routine stuff. Emma kept notes which she would type up later and pass round. There were a number of items of change to systems and once he had spoken, Madoc closed his diary.

'I assume there's nothing else?' he said, almost as an afterthought.

'You said I would have a week's trial and then review my position here,' Nick stated.

'Oh yes. Well. I doubt I could find anyone else so I assumed you'd like to stay for a while. At least till we have news of Doctor Lavers' progress.'

'Thank you. Yes, of course I'd be willing to stay on. I love it here.'

'Good. That's settled. Anything else?'

'If I am staying, I'd like to suggest one or two new things. I mentioned some of them during the week. Leaflets and so on. I think they would be informative and useful tools to educate. People can read them while waiting and it's amazing just how much information might stick in their minds.'

'Many reasons not to. They'll all believe they've got every disease under the sun if they read such stuff.'

'I think it's an excellent idea,' Emma said. Madoc gave one of his classic grunts and said it would be up to her to keep the place tidy when people discarded them.

'I also wondered if I could hang a few pictures or photographs around the place. It's all a bit bleak and bare. Some nice pictures would make the place more welcoming and pleasant to sit while they wait.'

'We have enough trouble getting them out as it is. You'll be suggesting putting in water machines and coffee on tap next. Sorry, but there's no budget for such niceties.'

'I can print some of my own photographs off on the computer and I don't mind buying a few of those glass frames.'

Madoc stared at her as if she'd gone mad but he gave a shrug.

'Do what you like,' he said grumpily. The two women looked at each other and raised eyebrows slightly and gave a small smile.

'Would you like another coffee?' Emma asked. They all nodded and sat for a while longer. Meeting over,

Madoc asked if they had plans for the weekend.

'I'm driving to Devon to see my parents and bring some more clothes and stuff down. I didn't bring too much to begin with in case it didn't work out. Thought I'd bring my surf board and wetsuit.'

'Terrible hobby. I've seen too many disastrous results even to want to watch.'

'I've had my share of bruises and bumps. But there's nothing like it. A real buzz when you catch a good wave.'

They argued light-heartedly, each realising that the other would never be swayed. Emma left them and went to type up her notes. Feeling on a bit of a high, Nick broached the subject of a computer for Emma to use. She offered to teach the secretary the basics and even to help her if it went wrong. Madoc looked slightly cross but gave in and said it was up to her.

'So, will you organise it?'

'A massive task to get patient notes

on to a system.'

'We could pay someone to come in and do it for us. Save hours in the long run.'

'I'll think about it over the weekend. Costly business though. And I'm not sure Emma would even want to contemplate the idea.'

'I think she will actually. She mentioned that her wrists and fingers are aching after a long typing session. A computer is so much less effort.'

'You're a strange one,' Madoc said suddenly. He gave her one of his rare smiles. Nick couldn't help thinking he should do it more often. He actually looked quite handsome when he did smile. She raised an eyebrow at his comment. 'Why should you care so much? I haven't exactly been very welcoming and your stay here is only temporary.'

'Maybe. I just like to see efficiency and something to make life simpler.'

'You've done well here this week.'

'For a woman.'

'Now I never said that.'

'Of course not. But thanks for the compliment.' She paused, wondering if she might question him about his hatred, or was it fear? of females. 'Why do you have such a problem with us?' He looked distinctly unhappy.

'By us, you mean the female race?'

She nodded, grinning at his suggestion they were actually a race apart.

'Not something I can talk about. Bad experience in my life. Maybe one day I might tell you. Depends on where . . . never mind. You can get off a bit early this evening if you like. I assume you're driving up to Devon this evening?'

'Thanks. That was the plan. What happens with weekend duty? Do we take it in turn?'

'We have an out of hours arrangement. I only answer special calls. Like my patients at the Beeches. I don't have many hobbies so it is rarely a problem.'

'Sounds as though you need to get out more. We'll have to see what we can organise in future.' She realised she had said far more than she intended and was rewarded by one of his special glares. Handsome had she thought? Not when he looked like that. An angry dark lion, a maned lion she thought. His mood could switch in seconds or perhaps it was simply that he had only a small range of expressions.

★ ★ ★

It was a restful weekend with her parents asking questions non-stop. What had happened to the Doctor Roskelly they had known and remembered with affection? What was the new one like? Was she getting enough to eat? What was her home like? How long was she planning to stay there?

'For goodness sake, Mum, I'm twenty-eight years old. I've been living away from home for years. And I have been far too busy working to give Madoc the third degree about his family.'

Wisely, her mother busied herself in the kitchen, knowing that she could at least ensure proper meals while her daughter was at home.

Nick began the following week with very much more confidence than the previous one. Emma continued sending most of the younger patients to her, leaving Madoc to deal with the older group. Being a village, there were certainly plenty of the latter. It was one of the reasons for Cornwall's health provision to feel stretched so often. The number of retired people was only exceeded in the summer months when holidaymakers poured into the county.

The kind of medical treatments changed during the summer, as they mopped up grazes from slipping on rocks, bumps and bruises from the surfers and sunburn, instead of arthritis and cold based infections.

Time went quickly and as the weeks passed, she had formed a routine. When her day was over, she had started to take long walks along the beautiful cliff tops. The following week, schools would be breaking up for summer and quiet cliffs would become crowded and peaceful evening walks would have to cease for a while.

Madoc began to accompany her on a few evenings and a couple of times, they had gone to the pub for an evening meal. Though they often talked about their work and patients' problems, he seemed to be relaxing in her company but Nick would be hard pressed to say she had grown any closer to him.

As for Madoc himself, he was rather enjoying having someone else around. He had rarely spent any time outside work with his other partner. Alan Lavers was much older than him and married with a teenage family and though he and his wife had invited him for occasional meals, Madoc found it difficult to enjoy a family life with three noisy children in the house. He felt slightly guilty about his lack of attention to them at their time of need and made a mental note to call soon.

He and Nick were planning a walk along the coast to the next village that evening and he was going to suggest they had a drink and possibly some food at the pub there. The landlord was one of his patients and had often invited him to call in.

Being essentially a shy man, Madoc had never taken up the invitation but with Nick as a companion, he might do so. He admitted to being impressed by the way she had settled down. He liked her ability to communicate with her patients, not to mention the fact that she had picked up on a couple of long term illnesses that his own failings had missed, partly through his own difficulty in talking to people.

Perhaps having a woman doctor in the practice was a good idea. Admittedly, there was a district nurse who shared her rounds with a couple of other villages and Emma was a good enough secretary-cum-receptionist but she was really rather overworked.

They strode along the cliffs that evening in companionable silence. 'I must do this more often,' he said when they finally stopped at the top of a steep climb. 'I need to get fitter. Perhaps I should get a dog to make certain I walk more.'

'Question of time really,' she replied. 'And once the place is filled with visitors, walking won't be such a pleasant experience.'

Once they'd both got their breath back, they set off again and soon arrived at the small yet delightful hamlet called Trevast.

'I thought we might have a drink here and a bite to eat. What do you think?' he asked.

'Fine, except I haven't brought any money with me.'

'That's all right. I have my wallet. Besides, the landlord is a patient, so he's hardly going to worry if we couldn't pay this evening.'

They sat outside the small pub, overlooking the tiny harbour.

'There must be dozens of little places like this around the coast. I think this county is unique and has so much variety. Newquay, with its big surf scene and loads of clubs and then the various towns around with plenty of shops and little places like this.'

'So which do you prefer?'

'Right now? This has it all for me. Bristol was great for a couple of years. Plenty to do and lots of arty things happening. But, I'm a peace loving soul at heart. Boring, aren't I?'

'Not in the least. Unusual though. Tell me about yourself. Apart from your quite impressive CV, I mean.'

'What do you want to know?'

'I gather there are no boyfriends around?'

'Not really. I have friends of course. Mostly ex-colleagues. I did have a fairly serious relationship with one of the anaesthetists but we both went our own way after a while. Now I'm foot-loose and fancy-free as they say.'

'You've certainly made an impact in such a short time, haven't you?'

'Just doing my job. I take it you're happy with my efforts then?' He nodded. 'Any news of Doctor Lavers?'

'Not much progress. I'm going round to see his wife later in the week. Oh, I forgot to say, I've ordered a computer for the office. We may need to send Emma on some sort of course.'

'Oh, that's excellent. I didn't like to mention it.'

'And there have been several favourable comments about your pictures. You have a talent for it.'

'I was pleased with them. I just have to splash some paint around my little consulting room and I'll be happy. I thought at the weekend, maybe?'

Madoc gave a sigh. He was beginning to feel as if he was on a roller coaster ride. Just how far did this woman intend to go?

'If you really must. I'm planning to be out a lot of the time. But you can let yourself in and do what you like. You do realise it must all be done and finished by Monday.'

'Of course. And we shall probably get busier next week. When the holidays really get going.'

Their food arrived and for a while, they concentrated on eating. It was a good enough meal, but not a patch on the pub in their own village. Madoc did open up a little as they ate and volunteered some information about his parents. After they retired a couple of years ago, they had bought a place in Spain and were enjoying life in a warmer climate.

'My father's arthritis is much better and they both seem much happier without the pressure of work. Mum often resented being an unpaid receptionist at home and never being able to get away from the practice. Things have changed now though with the whole system. With outside hours cover, we can at least get some quality time off.'

'My parents will be interested to hear

that. They were fond of your parents. I think they originally met through mutual friends. I always remember your father being very kind when I fell over once.'

'He was good with children. I never inherited his talent. In fact, the less I have to do with children, the better. I never want to have any children. I'd make a rotten father.'

'Lots of people say that. But when it comes to it, they discover talents they never realised.'

'Maybe, but I shall never find out. One of me was enough for them. Maybe if I'd had siblings it might have been different. But I simply will not have children of my own. Now, I'll go and pay and then we'd better start back if we're to make it before it gets totally dark.'

Nick sat staring out to sea. No children for Madoc, eh? She simply couldn't imagine ever making that sort of decision. She had always wanted children and the only thing stopping her was finding a suitable husband.

She glanced up at the sky. It had turned rather dark out to sea and there were threatening clouds rushing towards them. It was at least a two mile hike back, over rough ground. Maybe they should consider walking back along the roads. She put it to Madoc when he returned.

'It does look a bit dodgy. It's a long way by road though. Nearer four miles than the two of the coastal route. I suppose we could be wimps and order a taxi?'

'I'm a wimp of the first order,' Nick announced. 'Let's get a taxi. I'm feeling pretty shattered anyway. A glass of wine and a load of food and that's me done after a full day at work.'

They went back inside and asked the landlord for the number of a taxi firm.

'No need for that, Doc. I'll call my wife through to the bar and I'll drop you back. We've about done with food for tonight.'

'That's very good of you. I don't

want to trouble you. We can easily get a taxi.'

'Won't hear a word of it. I'm pleased to be able to help. You've always been good with my old mum in the Beeches so I do feel I owe you.'

'Oh, yes of course. I'd forgotten your mother was there.'

★   ★   ★

Within ten minutes, they were almost back at Gwillian. The rain was pouring down and the windscreen wipers working overtime. Nick was dropped off at her cottage and Madoc was driven up the hill to his own place.

She got inside and shook herself off. Her anorak was soaked in just the few seconds it took her to get out of the car. She felt very grateful to the friendly man and glad to be home unscathed. The walk back along the cliff tops would have been a disaster and potentially quite dangerous. It was a salutary lesson.

She felt that she had got to know a little more about Madoc this evening. He hadn't quite admitted his real problems but there was time. He certainly was an attractive man in so many ways. She might have allowed herself to have feelings for him, if it weren't for the one major drawback. No children. She couldn't bear to think of a marriage without children.

'Hey, Nick. Hold on there. Whoever was talking about the M word?' she said out loud. What was she thinking about? Still, she had some news to pass on to her parents about his family.

★ ★ ★

At work the next day, Emma mentioned that it was Madoc's birthday the following week.

'I was wondering if we should get him a cake or something? What do you think?'

'Why not? Maybe Auntie Dotty might like to come round as well. We could have it after we finish afternoon surgery.'

'What a good idea. Oh yes, I should also say thank you for the new computer that is arriving tomorrow. He's asked for the man to install it all and show me what to do. I must say, I face it with a mixture of dread and excitement. Suppose I can't use it?'

'You'll be fine. There are bound to be a few hiccups but you can take it steadily. You'll still have your old typewriter handy if it goes wrong. And I'll help you till you get it sorted.'

They chatted for a few minutes and Nick did her best to calm Emma's nerves. It seemed she had been attending some classes run at the village hall so she was at least familiar with the basic controls. At least the next day was Madoc's morning to be at the other surgery so Emma could have some time on her own to familiarise herself with the new set-up.

'So, will you invite Auntie Dolly to come for tea on Thursday next week?'

'Of course. I need to pay some rent anyway so I'll call in later. What about the cake? Where do I go for that?'

'I'll see to that. The baker does splendid cakes.'

Nick walked down to Auntie Dolly's cottage when she had finished. There had been only a few patients that afternoon so she finished early. She tapped on the door and heard Auntie Dolly call her to come in. Presumably, the old lady's second sight had told her who was at the door, she reflected.

'I'm just making some tea, if you'd like a cup.'

'Thank you. That would be lovely.'

'This is a herbal mix of my own. Should relax you.'

'Not too much I hope. I have to drive later on.'

'You'll be fine my dear. Now tell me, how are you getting on with that nephew of mine?'

'We're working quite well together, despite me being a woman. We've also been out for a few walks and shared some meals. But I expect you know all that.'

Auntie Dolly nodded.

'He's very up-tight about females though. And he won't talk about it,' Nick continued.

'He will when he's ready. I expect that Emma Liddicoat has put you in the general picture. Be patient, girl. He'll come round, mark my words. Maybe I should give you one of my potions to feed him. You can mix it with his food next time you eat together. Never fails.'

'I couldn't possibly, thanks all the same. If he wants to talk, he'll either do it or he won't. I wouldn't want to think he would only talk with the help of some potion or other. What do you put in it anyhow?' She was slightly intrigued to think what could possibly have any magical effect on anyone.

'That's my secret. Wouldn't do to tell anyone my secrets now, would it?' She gave a chortle, pretty close to a cackle of delight. 'They do work, you know.

My love potions are renowned. Many of the marriages in the area are down to my love potions. Guaranteed to bring happiness.'

'So why didn't it work for Madoc and his wife?'

'Never tried it. She was a piece of work.' Nick blinked at the slightly modern sounding phrase coming from the old woman. It seemed strangely out of place. 'Never should have married her. I told him at the time, but he was always stubborn. Now you, that's a different matter. I can tell you're the right sort of girl for him.'

'But you know nothing about me.'

'Don't you believe it. You'd be surprised what I can tell about you. I've looked in my books.' And your crystal ball no doubt, Nick thought with a giggle.

'Yes, I do have a crystal ball too,' Auntie Dolly said with a grin. Nick was startled. Seemed it wasn't safe even to think things in the presence of this one. 'But I don't talk about it too much. People scoff at such things these days. But the old ways you know. The old ways.' She paused and sipped her tea. 'Now, if you've come about the rent, it's already paid for. Madoc has settled it himself. And if you're going to invite me to a birthday tea with my boy, then I accept.'

'Is there anything you don't know?' Nick asked.

'Not a lot.' She gave another of her witch-like cackles. 'Let me know if you change your mind about my love potion. All quite harmless but very effective.'

'Thanks, but I won't change my mind. Thank you for the tea. I'll see you again soon. Three-thirty on Thursday.'

'I'll be there. You will be the right one. Mark my words. With or without my help.'

Nick said goodbye and left the witch's cottage, as she had come to think of it. It was all very silly really and she didn't believe in any of it. It was however, slightly disconcerting to discover that she knew so much. After all, they had only planned the birthday tea party a few minutes before she had come down to visit Auntie Dolly.

* * *

Nick had decided it was time for a supermarket shop. She felt slightly guilty not supporting the village shops but there really were a number of things she needed to have in stock. They were not available in the village, though Maggie had offered to buy in anything she wanted. Truth to tell, Nick felt in need of a wander round a large store and drove off to the nearest town.

She filled a trolley with packets and jars and added a couple of bottles of wine, along with the non-alcoholic things she had bought in case she entertained Madoc again. She put in a small collection of frozen foods but was limited by the size of her small freezer. The fruit and vegetables she would still buy from Maggie, partly to free her conscience and partly because they were fresh and locally grown.

Though she never claimed to be much of a cook, there were some things she enjoyed making and now she had the right ingredients.

She also picked up a birthday card. It had a large lion on the front and she couldn't resist it. Madoc may never understand the significance of it to her, but at least it represented his birth sign of Leo. She glanced at her watch. She should get back to Gwillian. It was her late surgery this evening and she had to allow time to unpack her shopping.

She hoped nobody would notice her unloading the car and then felt rather silly. Even the doctor was allowed to go outside the village sometimes.

She stowed away her purchases, changed her blouse and picked up her medical bag. She strolled up the hill and arrived in good time for the next round of patients. She told Emma that Auntie Dolly had accepted the invitation for tea the next week.

'Is this a traditional thing you do?' Nick asked.

'Well no. We haven't done it before. But having another female here, it seemed a nice idea. Why do you ask?'

'Auntie Dolly seemed to be expecting her invitation.'

'She's a law unto herself,' Emma laughed. 'Likes everyone to think she has special powers. I'll admit she has an uncanny knack for knowing some things but I suspect she's just a very observant lady who can put two and two together.'

'Maybe. What about these love potions she talks about?'

'A clever lady. She can put the idea into your head and leaves it to your own psychology to sort it out.'

'I suspected as much. Now, I'll go and sort myself out. You all ready for your big computer day tomorrow?'

'Not sure. I love the idea of not having to press so hard on the old keys. My fingers ache some evenings. I guess I'll manage, though I'll be grateful for your help.'

The door opened and the first patient came in.

Nick Meets An Old School Friend

Nick arrived early the next morning, ready to help Emma sort out her desk for the new computer's arrival. They had arranged a table beside her desk for the appointments book and the type-writer. It would take a little time to install everything and they still had to keep everything going as normal.

'Oh, bless you,' Emma said as she bustled in. 'I meant to sort things out last night but I was in a bit of a state in the end. I was a bit late getting home to put our evening meal on. Derek does like to eat on time or he says he gets indigestion.'

Nick realised this was the first time she had mentioned a husband and for some reason, she had assumed Emma lived alone. She felt guilty that she hadn't even asked about her private life. The patients began to arrive so Nick went into her consulting room to begin the day. She heard noises coming from the waiting-room and realised the computer had arrived. When she had finished with her patient, she went to see what was happening before the next one came in.

'Everything all right?' she asked. Emma was looking troubled.

'I hadn't realised there would be so many boxes. I don't think I'll ever manage it all.'

'You'll be fine. Dave here will sort it all out and show you the basics.'

'Mornin', Doc,' said the young man. ''Bout time you got into the twenty-first century here. Don't worry. I'll have it all up and running in no time. The other doc said you wanted programmes to run your appointments and fairly basic word processing. That right?'

'Correct. Will you be able to explain it to Mrs Liddicoat?'

'Course I will. We've known each

other for a long time, haven't we, Emma? I've been taking the classes she's been attending. Doing very well. She's a natural.'

'That's wonderful,' Nick replied. 'Fine. Well, I'll leave you to it. Mrs Fletcher, Maggie. Please come through. Do sit down. Now, how can I help?'

Maggie explained her symptoms. She was having pains in her right elbow and finding movement becoming restricted.

'Do you have pain anywhere else? Your shoulder for instance or other joints?'

'No, not really. It's been aching for a while but last night I could hardly bear it. Just got worse after I'd finished putting up the orders. Probably just overdoing it a bit. Only I thought I ought to get you to look at it. I have to work all hours to keep the shop open and running. Competition's pretty stiff these days and the older residents do rely on me.'

Nick felt a pang of guilt about her shopping trip.

'I suspect you've got bursitis. It's a joint inflammation, possibly brought on by overdoing things a bit. You're going to have to rest it for a couple of weeks. And take ibuprofen. I assume you don't have any problems with ibuprofen?'

'Not that I know of. But I don't see how I can rest. Not with the shop.'

'Haven't you got someone who can help you? What about Tommy? Won't he be home from school, for the summer?'

'He'll want to be off out all the time. Meeting his friends and all.'

'Well, you really do have to get some help. Maybe he could pack your orders and lift the heavier things before he goes off out with his friends. Tell you what, I'll give you a crêpe bandage for it. Not strictly necessary and may not help much but if your family and even some of your stronger customers see it, perhaps they'll take pity on you. Use a bit of psychology.' She thought of Auntie Dolly and her love potions as she spoke and smiled a little.

'All right. Well thank you, Doctor. Oh

dear, I could do without this just when the season's getting going. Two weeks, you said?'

'Probably. If you take it easy. I won't give you a prescription. It will be cheaper for you if you buy the ibuprofen at the chemist.'

Maggie left the room and Nick's next patient came in. She wrote up the notes and looked forward to being able to type them into the keyboard. That was some time away yet but it was a good thought.

★　★　★

At lunch time, Dave was still working away with Emma watching intently. Madoc returned from his morning clinic and stood over the reception desk, looking anxious.

'I hope you're going to manage this, Emma.'

'She'll be fine, Doc,' Dave assured him. 'She's my star pupil. Give her a week and she'll have the whole thing running like clockwork. And she's got my phone number if anything goes wrong. Now, show me how you can manage the booking chart.'

Emma smiled nervously and sat down in front of the keyboard. Hesitantly, she pressed the keys rather too heavily but managed to get the chart showing on the screen. 'Excellent. Now, Mrs Bloggs wants to see Doc Roskelly at ten o'clock tomorrow. Put that in.'

Carefully, Emma typed it in. 'Right and now Mr Smith wants to see the other doc at four o'clock on Friday.' He gave her a number of other tests and she completed them all, even when an appointment was already taken. She quickly managed to find an alternative and it really looked as if it was working well. Madoc nodded his approval and went through to the kitchen.

'Oh dear. I'm so afraid I shall forget something. Maybe I shall keep a written note for a while until I'm certain it's all working.'

'Write the basics on one of those sticky things and put it on the side of the monitor. Then when you're sure how it works, take it off and soon, you'll be a 'sticky thing' free zone,' Nick suggested. 'It worked for me when I first started. Sorry to interrupt, but have you got my home visiting list for this afternoon?'

'You've only got the one. Up at Gower Farm. One of the children's ill. Something with an infected wound on her leg. The mother didn't think it was anything much but wanted her checked out. She couldn't get the child down to the surgery so I said you wouldn't mind calling in.'

'Fine. I'll just get a sandwich and be on my way.' Madoc came through from the kitchen.

'I've got some salad and a few things for lunch if you'd like to join me. Save you going home.'

'Thanks. That's very kind of you. I was going to make a sandwich.'

'I can do better than that. Come on

through. We'll leave Emma to her battle.'

'I think she's doing pretty well actually. Don't underestimate her determination. She's striking a blow for womankind.' Madoc treated her to one of his glares and she grinned.

It was a pleasant interlude, sitting at Madoc's kitchen table eating fresh rolls and salad with a piece of locally produced Cornish Brie. They washed it down with mineral water and chatted amiably about their patients and the new computer.

At present, the plan was to use it simply for letters, appointments and various administrative tasks. Putting patient records on to it would take a long time but as Emma became more proficient at using it, she would be able to type them in gradually.

'You know, when you relax, you're a very different person,' Nick told him. 'In fact, I do suspect you're beginning to treat me as an equal rather than someone from an alien species.' She had felt a sudden rush of tenderness towards him and wanted to show that all women weren't like his ex-wife. His glare made her pause and then to wish she hadn't said anything at all.

'I'm glad you feel more at ease,' he replied and then stopped himself. He had almost smiled but instead, he rose from the table and concentrated on making coffee. He couldn't possibly allow her to think that he might really be softening. Never, never again would he allow himself to be taken in by any woman. 'You are certainly proving yourself as a good doctor but don't forget this is a temporary position. Don't get too settled. I'm planning on visiting Alan Lavers soon. I shall be able to get some idea of how long it's likely to be before his return.'

'Yes, of course. I hope he's doing well. From my own point of view, sorry as I shall be when he does return, it must be a very difficult time for him and his family.'

'Absolutely. Now, I should move on.

Patients to call on.'

'Thanks very much for the lunch. Maybe we can have supper together? It's my turn to pay if you fancy a meal out somewhere.'

'I suspect we're seeing a bit too much of each other. You must have other things to do. People to see.'

Nick felt as if she had been slapped in the face. Just when she thought they were getting on so well. In fact, just when she could begin to admit she was beginning to like him a lot, despite some of his attitudes.

Well, clearly she had been wrong. She was simply proving herself to be useful to him. Despite everything she had been planning for the practice and for her own future here as a doctor, it seemed she was merely whiling away a few weeks until his partner returned.

She would see what was said about Doctor Lavers' progress after Madoc's visit and consider moving on. This was not the time in her life to get close to someone and then find herself rejected.

No, it was quite clear. Any softening towards him or any deeper feeling, must stop right now. Any gestures he might make towards her, meals shared, the companionable walks were never meant as a sign that he enjoyed her company. Most likely, he was tying to make sure she stayed for as long as he needed her, for her skills as a medical practitioner. She felt oddly depressed at the thought.

*　*　*

On Thursday, she propped up her card on Madoc's desk. She had pondered long and hard about a suitable gift for him. She wanted to acknowledge his birthday with something more than a card but found it difficult to think of anything he might like.

In the end, she had settled on a book of coastal walks, beautifully illustrated and not so expensive that he would be embarrassed. She was giving that to him later in the day. Emma had brought in a delicious looking cake which was stored in the fridge and had made sure there was extra milk for tea. She was enjoying her new computer and seemed to be managing everything remarkably well.

Promptly at three-thirty, Auntie Dolly arrived. Madoc was in his consulting room, catching up on notes. Nick and Emma had set out a tea-tray and put the cake in the centre of the table. The outer door was locked and two wrapped presents were waiting beside the tray. Nick was sent to knock on his door.

'Can you come through?' she asked.

'I'm busy,' he grunted.

'Well, it will have to keep for a while. You have a visitor.'

He sighed and got up, looking annoyed by the interruption.

'Oh, Auntie Dolly. What are you doing here? You are all right, aren't you?'

'Happy birthday, my boy. Thirty-three today.'

He looked embarrassed and very

116

uncomfortable. The other two joined in with good wishes and Emma handed him a knife to cut his cake.

'Goodness me. Very kind of you, but I don't usually acknowledge birthdays.'

'I thought it would be nice to change that,' Emma told him. 'Especially having Nick here with us.'

They all chorused happy birthday as the cake was cut. Nick handed him her gift and he looked even more embarrassed. However, he accepted it gratefully and unwrapped it.

'That's beautiful. Thank you very much. Most kind of you. I'll have to take a few more walks and see the sights for myself.' Nick noticed that he didn't suggest that 'we' might take more walks. Never mind, she thought. She wouldn't be here for much longer. Emma had bought him the inevitable socks, saying you could never have too many socks.

'I'll have your supper ready later,' Auntie Dolly informed him. 'And you're invited too, Nicola.'

'Thank you but it's not necessary. I'm sure you'd like to have your nephew to yourself for once.'

'Nonsense,' the old lady replied. 'You two need sorting out. I'll have to take steps.' Madoc looked terrified at the suggestion and rather angry.

'Thanks, Auntie Dolly. But you keep your wicked ideas to yourself. None of your herbal concoctions thank you very much. I'm not in the market for any of your strange ideas about me or my future.'

She gave the inevitable cackle.

* * *

Nick felt extremely nervous about the supper invitation but couldn't think of any excuses to refuse it. They finished the cake and settled back to their various tasks. Auntie Dolly trotted off down the hill, remarkably sprightly for her age, not that any of them knew exactly what that might be. At six-thirty, as instructed she walked to

Auntie Dolly's cottage. Madoc was already sitting in the little room, making it look half its size with his large frame.

'So, explain the significance of the lion on the birthday card,' he demanded when she was sipping what Auntie Dolly assured her was a nonalcoholic cordial of her own making.

'Leo. Your birth sign,' Nick said carefully.

'Right. Nothing to do with my bad temper then? I mean, no suggestion that I roar when I'm bad-tempered?'

'Of course not. Could it be that I think you're something of a pussycat underneath?' Nick bit her lip. What on earth had made her say that? She glanced at the cordial and wondered if there was something in it that had loosened her tongue.

Madoc glared at her. What was it about this woman that intrigued him so much? He gave her a smile that was enough to melt ice and she felt a warm glow. If she hadn't known better, she might have interpreted his smile as an apology of some sort. Just where did she stand with this man? Mixed messages all the way.

'Come on through.' Auntie Dolly instructed. They obeyed and delicious smells rose from the bowls on the table.

'Oh good. Your summer vegetable soup. Delicious. Thank you,' Madoc exclaimed.

They ate a wonderful supper of very freshly caught fish and a herby salad and finishing with local strawberries and cream. It was the perfect summer meal. Auntie Dolly was certainly an excellent cook.

'Now, I know Madoc won't drink coffee at this time of night but I can offer you some, my dear.'

'I won't, thank you. It does tend to keep me awake. That was a lovely meal. Thank you so much for inviting me.'

'Now I suggest you two young ones take a little walk to aid digestion before you sleep. Get away with you now. I'm getting old and need my sleep too.'

'At least let me help with the washing up,' Nick offered.

'Certainly not. I shall potter on in my own time. Besides, there isn't room for two in my tiny kitchen. Go on, it's a nice enough evening and still light.' She shooed them out of her cottage and obediently, they walked down the hill to the harbour.

'I apologise for my aunt, if she embarrassed you. She gets these ideas and sometimes there's nothing you can do or say to stop her or change her mind. I must assure you though, I have no . . . I don't know how to say it.'

'No dishonourable intentions? Or even honourable ones.'

'I suppose that's what I mean. Sorry.'

'No worries. I'm here as a doctor. I'm not looking for a relationship or anything else. Just want to do a good job.'

'Thanks for understanding. Now, shall we go up the hill on the other side or do you want to call it a day?'

'Walk for a bit. I feel very full and need to get some air before I settle down.' It was a beautiful evening and the sun was setting over the sea, making orange streaks across the water and a glorious azure blue line along the horizon. 'That is such an amazing colour,' Nick exclaimed. 'Almost indescribably beautiful.'

'Cornwall truly manages to produce some magnificent spectacles. Now, I think I'd like to get back home. Thanks for helping make this a special birthday.' He touched her arm as he spoke and she felt a pleasant thrill. At her door, he gave her a peck on the cheek. She felt confused and knew she was blushing. He was certainly a master of mixed messages.

'Good night,' she stammered and pushed open her door.

'Night. See you tomorrow.' It had been quite a day.

★　★　★

Saturday was wet. Nick drove to Truro and spent time wandering round the shops. It was rather busy and after buying a couple of new T-shirts, she decided that Gwillian was a much nicer place for her current mood. She felt restless and unsettled in her mind. She even contemplated going to work and typing a few patient details into the computer but decided against it as it might interrupt Madoc and seem as if she couldn't entertain herself, which of course, she couldn't, she decided.

* * *

The next day was perfect. The sun shone down from a cloudless sky and she looked out to sea, noticing there were some good waves. Impulsively, she dug out her old surfboard and wetsuit and drove round to the next cove where the beach was safe for surfing. There were several youngsters there and immediately, she felt too old to be doing this. All the same, she went into the water and soon joined the row of black clad folks waiting for the perfect wave. She realised it had probably been too long since her last outing and watched as the others skilfully stood up on their boards.

She leant on her own and floated in on her stomach. She paddled out again and the next time, caught a good wave that drove her into the shore with a huge rush. That was better. She watched the others still leaping up to work the water beneath their boards and made spectacular landings almost on the beach itself. She was too old, she decided and walked back up the beach. She unzipped her wetsuit and sat on her board to watch the others. An older couple of males walked by. One of them stopped to speak to her.

'You're new around here, aren't you? Holiday or local?'

'Temporarily a local. I'm working here for the summer, at least.'

'Welcome to Cornwall.'

'Thanks. Actually, I used to live in Cornwall for many years so I'm really back on familiar ground.'

'You didn't go to school in Truro did you? You look sort of familiar.'

'Well yes. But . . . '

'Paul Allingham. I suspect you were in the year below me. Didn't you go to Uni . . . medical school, I seem to remember.'

'Wow. I'm impressed. What a memory. Yes, I'm a fully-fledged doctor.'

'Yes, Nick. And you're doing locum work for Doc Roskelly.' Paul's companion nudged him and indicated they needed to be moving on. 'Sorry. We're meeting someone. See you around maybe?'

'I'm sure we shall. Nice to see you again. Bye.' Nick smiled and raised a hand to wave. She searched her memory . . . Paul Allingham. Yes, he was a prefect in the year above her. Very sporty and very popular with the girls in her year. A long time ago. It seemed like another life altogether. But then, it was.

★   ★   ★

It began as a fairly routine week the next week. There were the usual holidaymakers with assorted problems. Cuts and grazes, stings from bees or wasps that had provoked an allergic reaction and one broken arm which was dispatched to the hospital for plastering.

On Wednesday just before lunchtime, a call came in from the local lifeboat crew. They had been called out to one of the local fishing boats where a fisherman had been injured when the boat's engines had failed. Evidently, it was too near to the cliffs and the helicopter air ambulance couldn't get close enough. There was an on-shore wind preventing them from lowering anyone down so the inshore lifeboat had been summoned. They daren't risk waiting for the fishing boat itself to be rescued.

'Can one of the doctors come out with us?' they asked.

Emma was troubled. She hardly liked to ask Nick but she knew Madoc wouldn't want to go. He came into the room and asked what was the problem. Emma explained and Madoc went quite white.

'Do you think you could do it, Nick?' she asked. 'It's not an easy rescue. The sea's rough and it might be dangerous.'

'Well, yes I suppose so.' She glanced at Madoc and saw a flicker of relief cross his face. 'Is there a problem?'

'I'm . . . well, I . . . ' He was stammering and spluttering. Emma spoke out.

'He has a phobia about water.' Madoc clenched his fists and looked ashamed.

'It's stupid, but I can't swim well and have always hated water. But I shouldn't expect you to go so I'll just have to grit my teeth and do it.'

'I'll go,' Nick insisted. 'No problem to me. Really. I love the water and I'm sure the crew will take care of me. Now, any clues about the injury?'

'Not really. Maybe something broken, but they were concerned about his heart,

I think,' Emma replied.

'Right. I'll put a selection of medications in my bag. They'll presumably have oxygen?' She rushed to gather what she needed and almost ran down the hill to the harbour where the lifeboat was waiting. She was handed a life jacket and clambered into the slippery rubber raft. There were three crew members on board, one of whom she recognised immediately as Paul.

'We meet again,' he smiled at her as he perched on the narrow seat beside her.

'Didn't realise you were one of the lifeboat crew,' she shouted, her words lost in the wind that was whipping round them as they broke out of the protection of the harbour wall.

They bounced along over the waves and she concentrated on holding on tight to the various ropes around the outside of the craft. It suddenly seemed very small against the vastness of the ocean. They were heading straight for the high cliffs bordering the bay.

When they rose on the crest of a wave, she could see the fishing boat, alarmingly close to the sharp rocks. She closed her eyes swallowing back the fear that was rising. Madoc may be scared of the water but the water itself seemed to be the least of her worries at this moment. How on earth was she going to get from this bucking, heaving little boat into the fishing boat? And once she was on the fishing boat, how on earth would she be able to treat a patient? She felt Paul's hand grip her own and opened her eyes. He leaned right against her ear and shouted.

'Don't worry. I'll look after you. Promise.' She gave him a feeble grin and she clutched his hand gratefully in return. They had almost reached the fishing boat.

Madoc Feels A Pang
Of Jealousy

Somehow, the fishing boat had managed to get out an anchor which was just about holding them off the treacherous rocks. The lifeboat pulled alongside and expertly, one of the crew threw a rope up to the men on board. They were moored loosely to the rails on the sides of the boat and sent a couple of lifebelts down the craft. Expertly, Paul managed to attach Nick firmly into it and using some of the net hauling tackle, she was hoisted up to the deck.

It was all so quick, she had no time to be nervous and immediately was able to begin examining the injured man. He was pale but breathing reasonably well. His intense pain was obvious. Bouncing up and down on the waves made listening to his heart rather tricky but she decided there was time to tackle his injuries and then decide what to do next. She felt Paul arrive beside her and he shouted in her ear once more.

'I've got a radio connection to the helicopter. They say that if he's fit enough to wait a few minutes, we might be able to take the boat away from the cliffs and they can send down a winchman. The tide's turning and we're not being dragged towards the cliffs any more. They'll then take him to hospital.'

Nick nodded her agreement and examined his shoulder. It was clearly dislocated and the poor man was in agony. She managed to take out a dose of morphine and injected it into his arm. No way could she put in a cannula and prayed that she had been steady enough to get it to where it was needed. She shouted to Paul to tell him what she was doing and he communicated it to the helicopter pilot.

'I'm going to try and pull the shoulder back into place. Can you hold on to him and try to keep him still?' She shouted to her patient telling him what she was going to do. She lined herself up and began gently to feel along his arm to get exactly the right place. 'Can you see the helicopter?' she shouted at her patient in a small attempt to distract him. Then she gave a heave and pulled the whole arm to re-locate the bone in its socket. He yelled as the pain shot through him and then he relaxed again as it subsided.

'Pulse is racing again,' Paul said, still close beside her.

'Not surprised. You've done so well,' she told the injured man. 'I think now's the time to get the boat away from the cliffs.' She kept her stethoscope in place, listening anxiously to the heartbeat. She fitted the oxygen mask over his face and told him to breathe deeply and steadily.

The boat's engines roared into life again and battling the mountainous waves, they began to move painfully slowly. The lifeboat, with one crewman down, bounced along beside them.

They had loosened the mooring ropes so that they weren't pulled underneath the fishing boat.

Slowly, slowly they moved out from the shelter of the cliffs and the boat began to roll slightly. The pilot headed into the waves to try to stabilise it. All the time, he was talking into his radio headphones and she looked up to see the red rescue helicopter hovering closer. Her patient needed adrenaline but she was slightly nervous of giving it to him as they were shaking about so much. Hopefully, the helicopter crew would be in time.

Paul received a message through his headphones and nodded giving a thumbs up signal to the pilot of both the boat and the helicopter. He leaned towards Nick again.

'They're dropping the stretcher and the winchman at the same time. They'll get our friend strapped in and lift him into the 'copter.' His voice was comforting in her ear, even if he was shouting. She passed on the information to her patient and he nodded weakly. He was drifting in and out of consciousness and Nick was becoming more anxious as the minutes crawled by.

At last, the medic arrived beside her and she shouted out the details of her treatment and what she considered necessary. Very quickly, he and Paul had the patient strapped into the stretcher and with a quick signal to the hovering helicopter, they lifted the two men as they swung wildly in the wind. Seconds later, they were flying out of sight and away to the hospital.

'Well done,' Paul said. 'Hopefully, another life saved. Now we have to get you back to the shore.'

She looked down at the bobbing boat as it rose and fell over the waves and gritted her teeth. Paul went down first and stood balancing, waiting for her to be lowered. She hated the feeling of helplessness and she floundered down into the bottom of the dinghy.

Her medical bag was lowered down

to join her and the crew of the fishing boat all waved gratefully. What a tough life, she thought and made up her mind to show more respect to the next piece of fish that was put on her plate.

The noise of wind and waves made talk impossible until they were back in the harbour. In the shelter of the wall, it became like a totally different country.

'Thanks, Doc,' the crew said as she was helped out of the boat. 'Let's hope it was a good result.'

She stood on the jetty, her legs almost crumpling under her. She wasn't afraid of the water but she certainly knew the sea had to be respected. She had felt such a degree of helplessness out there. Everything was moving around so much that she had found her job difficult and prayed she had made the right decisions. The crew gave her a wave as they pushed off again and went round to the little lifeboat station round the corner.

Weakly, she walked up the hill to her

cottage. She wanted a hot drink, a shower and a change of clothes. She looked at her watch and saw it was almost time for evening surgery. Tough, she decided. Madoc would have to stand in. She opened her door and saw that Auntie Dolly was standing in her lounge. She gave a start.

'Sorry to intrude girl,' the old lady said. 'Saw you coming in and knew the best thing I could do for you was to have something hot ready and waiting. Sit yourself down and drink this. Don't worry. It's only hot chocolate. Hope you don't mind me coming in like this. I always keep a spare key just in case you ever lock yourself out.'

'Thanks,' Nick said feebly. She wasn't sure how she felt about the intrusion but right now, the hot chocolate was the most wonderful thing she ever remembered tasting.

'Now, when you've finished that, go and get yourself a hot shower. I'll call that nephew of mine and tell him you're safe home again but that he has to do evening surgery. You need to rest now.'

'Thanks very much. I'll do that. I must admit, I feel pretty shaken about.'

'And don't worry. I won't make a habit of coming into your home. It was just at this time in what I saw as an emergency.'

'Thanks again.'

★   ★   ★

A couple of hours later, there was a knock at her door. Madoc stood there.

'I've finished the surgery and we've had a call from the hospital to say your patient is fine. Seems he suffers from angina and should never have been out on the boat in the first place. He went because his uncle was ill and he didn't want to let down the rest of the crew. Forgot to take his medication with him. He then fell down and dislocated his shoulder. You did a splendid job in the circumstances. Well done.'

'Thanks, but I knew I should have

done more. It was just hard to communicate with all the racket of the wind and waves. I didn't want to do the wrong thing.'

'All is well. Now, I'm under orders from Auntie Dolly to make sure you have a proper meal. Can I tempt you to join me for dinner at the pub?'

'I'm shattered. Can I take a raincheck on it? I just want to slump down in front of something mindless on television. And I promise I'll eat something. I've got some frozen stuff I can microwave.'

'Not sure Auntie Dolly will settle for that but I understand. OK then, I'll see you in the morning. Take it easy now.'

After his visit, Nick sat down again and began to shake. She wasn't exactly cold but the tension of the afternoon suddenly hit her. She remembered her feelings of fear at different times . . . when she had seen the tiny fishing boat bobbing so close to the soaring cliffs . . . the jagged rocks that seemed only feet away . . . the height of the boat that she was going to be hoisted up to reach her patient. She felt tearful and almost wished she'd taken Madoc's invitation to share a meal. It was too late now.

She made another cup of hot chocolate, knowing this was simply the reaction to a very difficult and dangerous event. Amazing what chocolate can achieve she thought as she cuddled the mug in her hands. The shaking had stopped and she calmly went to look in her freezer to find something she could heat up for her supper. She actually felt very hungry now and took out a packet of curry.

* * *

Her dreams that night were filled with images of waves and she awoke feeling as if her bed was floating on the ocean. Once more she experienced panic at her memories and decided she needed to get up and maybe make a drink to break the cycle. Pathetic, she kept telling herself. Pathetic. Paul does this sort of thing all the time and he's calm about it. Whatever happened, she was not going to allow it to stop her going out on, or in the water. She would always have respect for the sea and would make sure she told the same thing to anyone else when the opportunity arose.

It happened sooner than she expected. When she arrived at the surgery the next morning, the phone was ringing. The answering machine was switched on as it was early and Nick heard the message come through on the speaker.

'This is a message for Nick Quenby. Doctor Quenby. This is Radio Cornwall. We understand you were involved in rescuing a sick fisherman yesterday and would very much like to do an interview. Please can you call us on 018 . . . ' Nick picked up the phone.

'Hello? Nick Quenby here. I heard your message.'

The presenter arranged for someone

to come and record an interview after morning surgery. Once she had put the phone down again, Nick began to wonder what she had done in agreeing to this.

It was more scary than going out in the first place. Madoc was pleased she had agreed.

'It's really good for the practice to let them know we do more than just sit in a consulting room. All down to you of course. I'm actually rather ashamed I let you go. I mean to take steps to cure myself of this stupid phobia. But, it's an opportunity to warn people of the dangers of the sea. It may look benign and pretty much of the time but it's a massive natural force that has its own agenda. I've seen all too many results of accidents that result from people thinking they can beat it.'

'I vowed never to take fish for granted any more. When you see what they have to go through to collect it.'

'True. But you know there are always plenty of people waiting to take up any places on crews when a vacancy occurs. It's in the blood of many families.'

'Thank heavens for the lifeboat services. We should have one of their collection boxes in the waiting-room.'

Madoc grinned and shook his head. 'You're a remarkable woman. Always thinking of someone or something you can help.' He went into his own room and she was left with a warm glow from his words of approval.

Emma arrived and wanted to hear all about the rescue. She oohed and aahed and said she felt nervous for Nick regarding the coming radio interview.

'I'll get some fresh biscuits to have with coffee, shall I? Or perhaps I should find time to pop down to the bakers and get something special.'

'I'm sure just coffee will do fine. I expect they'll be in a hurry. Now, I'd better get on or I won't be ready for the patients.'

★ ★ ★

The morning seemed much busier than usual with everyone wanting to talk about her gallant efforts. In the end she told everyone to listen to the local radio when she would describe things as much as she could. When she had finally seen the last patient she went into the waiting-room.

Emma handed her a list of phone calls that had come in. Two of the local papers wanted a picture and an interview and there was a message from some male called Paul who wanted her to call him back and left a number. She blushed slightly as she read it and Emma was curious.

'So, who's he? Some secret admirer?'

'No. Nothing like that. Actually, he went to the same school as me and he's one of the lifeboat crew. I expect he wanted to thank me or something. Mind you, the more I think about it, the less I actually did. I was terrified.'

'Makes it even braver. Anyway, you're quite the media star here today. Shouldn't be surprised if the television people don't come down. Everyone wants a story with drama and a happy ending.'

'Heaven forbid. I'm nervous enough about the radio. Television would be the end for me. Oh dear, looks like it's all happening. Here comes the radio interviewer.'

A pretty young woman clutching a clipboard and tiny recorder came into the waiting-room. Even to Nick, she looked about fifteen.

'Hi. I'm Daisy from Radio Cornwall. We appreciate you giving us your time. Is there somewhere quiet we can go to record a short interview?'

'We can go into my room.'

In Nick's consulting room, she asked if the computer could be turned off and rearranged the chairs. She explained about her recorder and told Nick how she wanted to conduct the piece.

'I'll ask you questions but my voice won't be heard when the piece is aired, so you need to sort of answer the question making clear what I'd asked.

Do you get what I mean?'

'Yes, I think so. Sounds a bit like exam questions when you have to state what you're answering.'

'And don't worry if you say the wrong thing. Editing is really easy these days with a computer.'

Nick spoke to the two local papers and told her story once more. They both asked if a photographer could visit and persuaded her that it was essential to the story. She demanded that the lifeboat crew should also have their photos taken as they were much more important than her but had to let it go.

Once all that was over, she fingered the remaining number left on her paper. Paul. Paul Allingham. She wondered why he had really called. It was a mobile number so she dialled it.

Maybe he was at work and couldn't answer it. She was right that he was at work but he did answer.

'Hello? Is that Nick?'

'Hi Paul. I'm just returning your call.'

'Great. Look, I can't really talk now

but I wondered if you'd fancy coming out for a drink with me one evening?'

'Oh. Erm . . . well yes, why not? When were you thinking of?'

'Tonight?'

'I suppose so, yes, that would be nice. Where shall I meet you?'

'I'll pick you up. Say seven-thirty? We can have something to eat if you fancy that.'

'OK. Thanks. Sounds good.'

She heard a muted cheering in the background. Evidently his success in asking for a date had been overheard and approved. She realised she knew next to nothing about him and hoped she wasn't making a mistake. She did feel slightly guilty about Madoc. But then, why should she? He had made it perfectly clear that he didn't want any sort of relationship and even if he did come round to it, there were to be no children . . . ever.

Such a pity. She still thought he was a lovely man, despite his faults. She went to pick up her house call list and found

Emma cursing gently as something had gone wrong with her computer.

'Can I help?' Nick asked.

'Oh, please. I wrote a whole load of things and pressed something and it all disappeared. Oh dear, I can't face doing it all again.'

'Have you saved everything as we went along?'

'I thought so. I was doing so well, really getting used to the machine and beginning to get braver in what I did. No fool like an old fool they say.'

'You're nobody's fool. Let me look. I dare say the files have found their way somewhere they shouldn't be.'

She sat down and pressed a few keys. She searched through various directories and found the file had been saved as she had thought, in the wrong place. It was soon back on the screen. 'No problems. It's just a bit like having a filing cabinet with lots of folders inside and a piece of paper gets put in the wrong place.'

'You can spend hours looking for it.

The computer is easier if you tell it to do the looking. I'll show you how to do it when we've both got a moment. Now, I must get on to my rounds.'

* * *

Nick was becoming familiar with the locality and was getting much more efficient as she drove out on her visits. Though the roads were busier with holiday traffic, she was learning short cuts and avoiding some of the congested routes. She parked outside a cottage where her patient lived and sniffed. There was a pasty shop across the road and freshly-baked pasties were scenting the air and were about to prove irresistible. Nick suddenly had her lunch planned immediately after she had visited Mrs Clements.

'Come in, Doctor. Door's on the latch,' called the occupant. Nick pushed open the door and went inside. It was her first visit to Mrs Clements and she sat down opposite to her. After a brief chat, she listened to her chest. All seemed well and her heart sounded steady and strong.

'What seems to be the real trouble?' Nick asked gently.

'It's this dratted arthritis. Suddenly got so painful I can hardly get out of my chair sometimes. I'm finding it all a bit much living on my own.'

'Do you have anyone to help you?'

'The lady comes from the social in the morning to get me up. She's scarcely got time to say hello though. That can be any time anyway. Some days I'm stuck there in bed till after nine o'clock or even later. Gasping for a cuppa by then I am. And I get the meals on wheels of course.'

'And don't you have any family who could help out?'

'They live up-country. One daughter and a son. They come down to see me sometimes but you know how it is. Busy lives and children always wanting to be taken somewhere.'

'I think we'll see if we can get you a

stay in one of the local respite care places. A couple of weeks maybe? Just to give you a break.'

'I'm not going into one of these homes. I've heard all about them.'

'Well, let's see if we get you a day there then. Just so you can see what it's like. Someone will collect you in the morning and bring you back during the afternoon. You might enjoy a change and some new people to talk to. Shall I see what I can do?'

'If you like. But I'm not moving in.'

'Of course not. I'm just suggesting a little holiday if you enjoy a day there. It might take a little while till there's a place but I'll try. Meanwhile, I'll try to get the district nurse to call in and I'll prescribe some pills to help with your pains. Is there anyone who can collect it for you?'

'Sometimes the chemist will deliver. But he needs the prescription leaving with him.'

'OK. I'll see to that.'

'You're new round here, aren't you?

Usually have that Doctor Roskelly. The young one. Nice young man but he doesn't understand. I liked the old one though. Charming man. I remember the young one being born, I do. His mother would have liked a whole load of babies but she could only have the one.'

Nick smiled, wondering how on earth she was going to get away from this lonely old lady. She desperately needed someone to talk to but Nick had other patients and it was already way past lunch time. She rose from her chair and tried to end the conversation as politely as possible.

'I'll be in touch when I have some news. Goodbye, Mrs Clements.'

'Goodbye, dear. Give my regards to Doctor Roskelly.'

She left, shutting the door carefully. It was worrying that the old lady had it left open all day but this was a busy village street so someone must keep an eye on her visitors. She went to buy her pasty and could hardly wait to drive somewhere quiet so she could devour it greedily.

She parked near the sea and bit into the wonderful pastry. Meat and potato, onion and turnip (or was it swede?) all blended together to make a touch of heaven in her mouth. It felt sinful to eat so much when she was probably eating out that evening but it was a rare treat. She wiped away the crumbs from her mouth and got out of the car to shake away the rest.

'You enjoyed that, didn't you?' called someone from the car parked next to hers.

'I certainly did. My first pasty in ages and I was famished.'

'Enjoy your day.'

'Thanks,' she called back and waved as she drove off. She hoped it wasn't someone who knew her. Not good for the image of a doctor who should be thinking of healthy eating. She had a few more calls to make and then it was time to get back to Gwillian for the later afternoon surgery. She hadn't seen

Madoc all day apart from first thing. She needed to discuss Mrs Clements with him. He was the expert in elderly care after all.

'Is Madoc in?' she asked Emma when she arrived back. 'Are you all right? You look quite washed out.'

'I'm fine. Didn't sleep very well last night. Anyway, Madoc's out. Back at The Beeches once more. I'm afraid another of his favourites is reaching the end. So sad. He does take it on so when he loses anyone but that's how it is.'

'Computer behaving itself?'

'It's lovely, thank you. I've even started typing up some of the patient notes. It's going to take an age but I expect I'll get there.'

'As long as there's a brief history and the medications they're on and anything else significant, that will be fine. We can always refer back to the old letters and notes if necessary.'

'Yes, I suppose so.'

'Would you like a cup of tea? I can

153

easily make it. There's nobody waiting for me yet.'

'You shouldn't have to do that. It's my job.'

'Nonsense. You take a bit of a rest. You'll be busy soon enough. How do you like it?'

'Milk and no sugar.' Nick realised it was the first time she had even made tea for the wonderful secretary who always looked after them so well. 'Any news of Doctor Lavers yet?' she asked as she put the mug beside Emma.

'Funny you should ask. Madoc's going round tonight. He asked me to phone and set it up. We should know a bit more tomorrow.' The first patient arrived and Nick went into her room.

By six-fifteen, she was finished and had made a list of notes for the following day. She locked up and set off down the hill to her cottage. It was windy and dark clouds were threatening once more. She had a shower and looked in her wardrobe for something to wear. It was all very casual, she

154

decided and pulled on some summer trousers and a silk shirt.

Paul was at least a year older than her. She was struck by a thought. Perhaps he was married. He'd always been sought after by the girls and somehow, seemed unlikely that he'd escaped everyone's clutches. She heard a car stop outside and looked through the window. A low sports model stood outside. She smiled. Just about what she might have expected. Trendy and very uncomfortable to get in and out. She hoped this wasn't going to be a totally disastrous evening.

'Well, hello again. You look gorgeous,' Paul said as he greeted her with a peck on the check. 'Bit different from the slightly drowned rat look when I last saw you.'

'I have had time to dry out since then,' she said lightly. She noticed Madoc's car drive past as she was clambering into the sports car and was too late to wave. He must have seen her though and she cursed. She didn't want to hurt his feelings and still felt guilty about turning him down last night. Too bad she told herself. He didn't own her and she was entitled to a life outside work without him.

'I thought we'd drive inland for a change. Nice little pub I know in the middle of nowhere. A lot of the gang go there so it's usually fairly lively. How does that sound?'

'Fine,' she murmured, thinking it wasn't exactly what she might have been expecting. Paul drove rather fast, though quite competently. She wondered if he intended drinking. It could be a problem. She decided to stick to soft drinks, just in case.

The pub was quite small and crowded. Several people called out to them as they arrived and soon, Nick was being introduced to so many people that she could remember none of them. There were a few girls among the crowd and they all gave Paul a kiss and hug as he passed them to get to the bar.

'I got you a white wine,' he said when he came back. I realised I forgot to ask what you'd like and as you see, it's a bit of a scrum. I can change it if there's something you'd prefer.'

'No, it's fine thanks. But I'll have soft drinks after this. Early start tomorrow and all that.' Paul had a pint of lager in his hand, she noticed.

'I'll get a menu next time. They do some good food here.'

'I'm surprised there's any room for eating.' She was practically shouting at him to make herself heard. This was not going to be a chatty evening. All the same, it turned out to be an amusing time.

They played bar billiards and table skittles with some of the others and laughed a lot, especially at everyone's inability to pot the balls. It was almost nine o'clock before food arrived. Nick was glad of her pasty lunch after all. It was after eleven when they got back to her cottage. She was certain Paul had drunk more than was legal and offered to drive them back to the village but of course, he refused.

'Nobody is allowed to drive my beauty,' he said. Nick cringed. Men and their cars, she thought. She said goodnight and thank you politely but he got out of the car outside her cottage. 'Aren't you going to invite me in for coffee?' he said pleadingly.

'I'm afraid I have an early start and it's well past my usual bedtime.'

'Oh come on,' he replied scornfully. 'You're not that ancient surely.'

'I have a responsible job to do. Lives depend on me being fully in charge.'

'And I don't?' Paul said with a touch of sarcasm.

'Of course you do. I'm sorry but I really am shattered and it's too late for coffee anyway.'

'OK. I get the message. See you around.'

'Thanks again. I had fun.'

He got back into his car and roared away much faster than was safe or necessary. End of something before it began, Nick decided. Too bad. It was no great loss to her. She seemed to have grown out of loud gangs together in pubs. He was quite a different Paul to the one who had looked after her so carefully when they were out on the boat.

★ ★ ★

'Did you have a nice evening then?' Madoc asked her rather stiffly the next morning.

'Yes, thanks.'

'Someone you've known for a while?'

'We ran into each other a couple of times recently. We went to the same school. He was on the lifeboat the other day and was very kind to me.'

'That's nice. Well, I suppose I should start work.'

'Actually, if you've got a minute, there are some things I need to ask about.'

They went into his consulting room and she took out her notes. She went through the various points and finally came to Mrs Clements. She explained the problem as she saw it and made her suggestions about some day visit for her.

'I know this is going to sound really dreadful but she is a difficult one. She's tried several of these days in various places and has always come away dissatisfied. Claimed that people didn't talk to her or look after her or bring her tea when she wanted it. Most places have refused to take her again saying there are other patients who really appreciate what they try to do.'

'She didn't mention any of that to me. In fact, she sounded quite pleased at the idea, as long as she didn't have to go and live permanently in any of them. But we need to consider getting her more care. She just sits in that chair alone all day.'

'She has a carer morning and evening. And meals on wheels. The nurse calls to bath her once a week. I know it's not much but it's the best funds allow.'

'She didn't mention any of that. But she did sent her regards to you and your father.' Nick couldn't help but laugh. She'd been taken in to some extent all the same, the poor woman didn't have a great deal of pleasure in life.

'I'll call in next time I'm that way. She flirts with me dreadfully. I can laugh it off but I find it a slightly difficult situation to handle. Most of them have their little ways but Mrs Clements is slightly different. Anyway, how was the radio interview?'

'Oh, I forgot all about it. It was on last night, I believe. Oh well. I'd have hated the way I sounded I'm sure. Right, I'd better get down to some letters and referrals. See you later.'

When she had gone from the room, Madoc gritted his teeth. He hated the fact she had gone out with someone in a flashy sports car. She wouldn't go out with him but had chosen to go out with some other man. He felt angry, annoyed and he realised, very jealous.

He had no right to feel jealous. He'd made it clear to Nicola that he wasn't getting involved with anyone ever again. He wasn't having children, he'd told her firmly.

The expression that flitted across her face at the time had indicated to him that she thought this was very peculiar. So why after all of that, was he at all concerned that Nicola was going out with anyone else? He hoped she was unaware of his thoughts.

In his strange mood, he'd also forgotten to mention his distressing visit to see his partner, Alan Lavers. He needed to bring her up to date about the situation, at the first opportunity. Meantime, there was another call he needed to make. He dialled the number from a business card.

'Bradford's Marina. How can I help?'

Nick Comes To A Decision

The summer weeks rolled quickly past and August Bank Holiday approached. Doctor Lavers was unlikely to recover sufficiently to return to work and Nick had happily agreed to stay on. She was always half expecting that Madoc would invite her to take up the partnership on a permanent basis but he had said nothing. She had been out with Paul again. He had phoned after their first date and apologised in case he had given the wrong impression. They had been out again on a couple of occasions.

She gathered that she was one of many women he took out but was happy with that as long as nobody else was hurt by it. He would never be anything more than a casual friend to her. The week before the bank holidays, Madoc surprised her by asking if she would like to go out on a boat trip with him at the weekend.

'Well, thank you. But I thought you didn't like water?'

'Can't say I do very much except in the bathtub. But, I was determined to get over it. I've been learning to sail. I've been having lessons for several weeks now and feel I can manage the dinghy quite well enough to risk taking you out with me. What do you say? Or perhaps you have plans to go out with your lifeboat man?'

'No plans at all. Thank you. That would be lovely. Shall I pack up a picnic?'

Weather permitting, the plan was to drive to the marina and sail out in a hire boat from there on the Saturday. It was further round the main bay and would open up an area she hadn't visited, including a part of the coast that couldn't be reached by road. It sounded great. It was a gorgeous day with light breezes and hazy sunshine.

She put her bikini on beneath long cotton trousers and a long-sleeved shirt. Even hazy sun reflected from the water could cause burning, especially to fair skin like hers. She put on her sun screen and pulled on a cap. The picnic was packed in a waterproof cold box that would stow beneath the seats. She hadn't sailed for ages and was really looking forward to it.

The dinghy they had hired for the day was the one Madoc had been using for his lessons and he felt confident he knew the layout. There was a mainsail and a jib, the smaller sail at the front of the boat. It was overall, about fifteen feet long, quite small and manoeuvrable but with a centre board that was pushed down into the water when stability was needed for certain conditions.

'Well done you for getting past your fears,' she told Madoc. 'I'm very impressed.'

'I felt so awful that day you went out

on the rescue. I was relieved when you said you'd go and then terrified in case you got hurt. I'd never have forgiven myself. There's me supposedly a strong man and you just a slip of a girl and I let you go. How could I do it?'

'You almost sound as if you really care.'

'Of course I care. How would it look if my locum was drowned in an accident I should have been attending myself?'

'I see.' She was slightly disappointed by his answer. 'So, are you happy if I sit back? Now the sails are set, I can be a lady of leisure.'

'Fine,' he said through gritted teeth. He tried hard to concentrate on everything he had been taught and was managing fine until a sudden squall hit them.

The sails flapped wildly for a moment and then filled again with wind and they scudded off in a different direction. White-faced, he hauled on the ropes . . . sheets he corrected himself mentally. Why ropes had to be sheets he would never understand. Sailing jargon he supposed.

'Shall I take in the jib?' Nick suggested, grabbing the appropriate sheets and pulling in the small triangle of sail at the front of the dinghy. 'It will make it smoother for you.' He nodded, clearly getting out of his depth. He gritted his teeth. Some show off he was. Nick was obviously much better at everything sporty.

'Do you think I could take the helm? It's ages since I sailed and I'm longing to have a go.'

'Course. Though I'm not sure how we change places.' His relief was palpable.

'Wait till the gusts settle a bit then you sit on the opposite side to the sails and I'll climb over you. Just don't let go of anything till I'm in place.'

The manoeuvre was carried out perfectly and Nick was soon in charge. She tugged in the sheets and soon had the sails correctly set. Madoc moved along and managed to become the perfect crew, sitting out when needed and down on the side struts as the wind lessened.

'Way to go,' Nick shouted in delight. She was loving it. 'I should consider getting myself a dinghy if I stay around long enough. So, where are we stopping for lunch?'

'Is it safe to sail closer to the land? We can look for a cove somewhere.' She nodded and turned towards the coastline. Immediately, the sails sagged and she pulled them in tighter. The nearer they were to land, the less the wind. They were drifting gently along when Nick spotted a sandy beach.

'How about that? Looks a clear run in. No rocks lurking just beneath the surface. OK, here we go. Pull up the centre plate.' She let the sheets go and the boat glided gently on to the beach.

'Brilliantly done. Think I certainly need a good few more lessons. Perhaps you can teach me. If you were serious about getting a boat, we could go halves on it and I can really become proficient. Now, where's this picnic you promised me?'

They flopped down on the sand and she unpacked the cold box. There was cheese and salads and various dips. With fresh baked rolls, it made a perfect summer meal. They washed it down with some locally made elder flower pressé.

'I'm going for a paddle,' she announced and kicked off her shoes. She tucked up her shirt and set off along the beach at the water's edge. Madoc watched her, thinking how lovely she looked, her slim figure and long, slender legs. He sighed, wishing things were different. That he was different. Damn that woman he'd married. It was all her fault.

Maybe it was time to tell Nicola all about it. This was the perfect time. They were relaxed and nobody else was around to interrupt them. He waited for her to walk back to him, preparing himself to speak of the one subject that he normally avoided at all costs. The small figure at the far end of the beach was almost out of sight. She was bending over something.

Suddenly she began to run back. She was waving at him and looked somewhat frenzied. She was shouting something but was too far away for him to hear. He got up and went towards her. He also began to run, wondering what on earth was wrong. She couldn't have hurt herself or she would hardly be running. She shouted again.

'Bring . . . first aid kit . . . Man . . . lying . . . there.' He could only catch part of what she was saying but it was enough to get the message. He ran back to the boat and pulled out the first aid kit from under the seat. It was pretty basic but better than nothing. He grabbed the life jacket too and a piece of tarpaulin. It would at least make a cover if needed. Nick was running back the other way now and he charged after her, clutching his collection of things.

Right at the furthest end of the beach, a broken surfboard lay on the sand, one end bobbing in and out of the water. The man had a huge lump already forming on his forehead and several grazes, some of them pouring out blood. His wetsuit was ripped across the chest and revealed several gashes beneath. He seemed to be unconscious. Nick was feeling for the pulse on his neck.

'He's alive all right and breathing steadily. He's quite cold. Must have been here for a long time. We'd have seen him if he'd crashed in where we were eating. To move him or not. What do you think?'

'Hi,' the man said, sitting up. 'Sorry ... I must have dozed off. Everything feels as if it's been battered and I just lay back and tried to relax my way through it.'

'We're both doctors. Just keep still please. I suspect that is a fairly superficial bump. Hopefully, there isn't any brain damage. Bumps on the front are often more visible but may be less harmful than on the back of the head.'

He felt expertly along his arms and legs while Nick looked at the gashes and grazes. She took out a bottle of sterile water from the kit and washed off the sand from the larger cuts. He lay still.

'Superficial again. I'll put some steri-strips across them and cover them loosely. It will all sting horribly.' She looked at Madoc, indicating that she wanted to speak to him out of hearing range of the injured man. 'Question is, what are we going to do with him? I've got a phone back at the boat. Can we get him into the boat do you reckon? If we sail just on the jib and stick close to the shore, we might make it to a village or something.'

'I don't think anything is broken but that's just on a cursory examination. Get your phone and see if there's a signal. If so, try for the air ambulance. Obviously, we can't leave him here so we'll have to move him.'

Nick ran back to the boat, her long legs covering the ground quickly. She found the waterproof pack she had stowed and took her phone out of the box. No signal. She held it high and turned around but the high cliffs behind were blocking any signal. She might pick one up out at sea but that would take too long.

She grabbed their belongings and climbed into the boat, giving it a hefty shove off the sand as she did so. She paddled it along the water's edge, horribly slowly it seemed but soon she could see Madoc with the young man now almost in a sitting up position. Thank goodness she muttered. Madoc had wrapped the life-jacket round him and that was keeping him warm. She leapt out of the boat, soaking her trousers as she did so.

'No signal,' she panted, trying the phone again at this end of the beach. 'Nothing.'

'This is Anthony. He was surfing alone and got caught in one of these hidden currents. Landed up on this beach, miles from where he started. No memory of where he is or which direction he came from.'

The young man looked white and closed his eyes, seeming to pass out. 'We need to find some way of getting him in the boat and lying down. Maybe if we could get him on to his surfboard or what's left of it and wrap him in this tarpaulin, he could lie across the middle of the boat. What do you think? Can you sail it like that?'

It was only a relatively small open dinghy with struts across the middle that could double as seats. It would cut off access to the centre plate and a more stable boat but they would need this space if the patient was laid over it on a surf board. The mainsail was down in the bottom of the boat and the boom, the long piece of wood that held the bottom of the sail, was pushed to one side and secured with the sheets.

'I'll give it a shot. You might have to paddle a bit to keep us stable.'

'No problem. Did you pick up our stuff from the beach?'

'I've dumped it down there. It's all a

bit damp but at least we've got it with us. OK, let's see what we can do. We need to use the other life-jacket to support his head. Just in case.'

'That means you won't have one to wear.'

'I'll manage. I can swim and if we're close in and the worst comes to the worst . . . I'm more worried about you though.'

'I can swim if I have to. Let's go.'

With Anthony seeming to drift in and out of consciousness, they slid his board beneath him and wrapped the tarp around him like a cocoon. Though he was fairly slight in build, it was still a dead weight and Nick was struggling to manage her end. The bobbing boat didn't help.

They got him in and then wondered where they were all going to sit. Madoc was quite well built and sitting on either edge was not an option for him if the boat was to be kept level.

'Right, you'll have to sit on the bottom at the stern end. It's wet and uncomfortable but it's the only way. You'll have to hold the tiller in place and I'll try to manage with the jib sheets.'

'Aye, aye captain. If I can get through this, I reckon I can become a sailor. But how do I paddle from here?'

'You don't. I'll have to manage somehow but I'll direct you with the tiller.'

'What's happening?' asked Anthony trying to sit up.

'Just try to lie completely still. We've got you wrapped up like a Christmas turkey so you don't have much choice. We're sailing along the coast till we reach the next village or till we can get a mobile signal.'

They progressed around each headland, hoping there was a village tucked away but there was nothing. Madoc kept trying the phone as he moved the tiller whenever Nick ordered him to. He could only just see over the sides of the boat and was very wet and beginning to get cold.

'Water sports. Who'd have them? Hey, I've got a signal. Feeble but it's there enough for an emergency call.' Quickly he dialled nine, nine, nine. Somehow, they seemed to work out roughly where they were heading from his description and the signal. 'One mile? OK, we'll be there as soon as possible. Get the ambulance standing by.' He switched off the phone. 'Seems we're about a mile from Porthaven. We must have been too far out to see it when we sailed past. They're sending the ambulance there. Air ambulance is on another shout but will come for us if needed.'

With the promise of an end in sight, they all rallied. Nick was far more anxious than she was letting on. She could see stormy clouds building behind them and white ripples on the water out to sea were an indication of a coming weather front. She hoped the boat hire company had decent insurance. She felt less than optimistic.

'Try to lean your weight over a bit,

Madoc.' She waved her hand to indicate the opposite side. The sheets were tugging in her hand and she let them go slightly. The small front jib sail loosened a little and filled again. They rushed forward. 'Push the tiller slightly towards the shore. Gently does it. Enough. OK. Keep it steady for a while.'

Poor Madoc was sitting with his back against the rear of the boat, bent sideways with the tiller close to his right ear. It was quite a sight. Nick was half in and half out of the boat, leaning out when she could to keep them moving but always anxiously watching the effect of the wind on the sail. She kept telling herself they were getting nearer their target but as yet, the village wasn't in sight.

The whole process was made more stressful by Anthony's groans. In some ways it was probably a good sign as it meant he was conscious. With a possible head injury, it was all very concerning. 'Round the next headland maybe,' she muttered.

As they cleared the point, a gust of wind caught the boat and they wobbled violently. Madoc lost his balance and let the tiller slide away from him. The boat spun round and Nick just managed to push herself back into the boat. She let the sheets loosen again and waited for Madoc to regain his place.

'Hang on to the tiller. Get it, Madoc.' He did so and she was able to regain control of the little jib sail. 'Close one,' she called out. The wind was definitely increasing. They needed to get closer to the shoreline as soon as possible. Things just couldn't get any worse or they would be in serious difficulties and could even lose their patient if he was in the water again.

She wasn't totally convinced that Madoc would be able to swim for long, especially without a life jacket. Maybe she should have insisted he kept it on and let Anthony's head rest on something else. Too late. She gritted her teeth and concentrated hard on keeping them moving and as stable as the sea allowed. Some relaxing day out this was proving to be.

'I think that's the village,' Madoc yelled triumphantly. It looked very small and still much further away than any of them would have liked. Their progress seemed snail-like with the wind beginning to gust round erratically. Nick began to think they might not make it safely without further help. 'I'm sure I can see a flashing blue light. Must mean the ambulance is there.' Nick turned to look.

'I think there's someone coming out towards us in a motorboat of some kind,' she said not without a degree of hope in her voice. Madoc rose slightly, knocked the tiller again and confirmed there was a boat. 'Tiller Madoc. Hold it steady,' Nick yelled.

'Sorry.'

The little motor boat was soon alongside. Two youngish men were in it and yelled to them.

'Throw your painter over and we'll

try to tow you in,' Nick leaned forward and managed to reach the mooring rope and tossed it towards the other boat. She couldn't get close enough to make a proper throw but they had a boat hook and managed to catch and hook it in. 'Hang on tight. It's not much of an engine to pull two of us in but we'll give it a go.'

Progress was painfully slow but they were getting closer to the shore. Soon they could see the people standing watching and several men waded into the water as they approached, all ready to help. Nick glanced at Madoc and saw him close his eyes in relief.

Once the boat was hauled up on to the sand, Nick loosened the sail completely and let it flap until the patient was lifted out of the boat. Cramped and stiff, Madoc hauled himself to his feet and began supervising as the paramedics came from the ambulance and examined Anthony. With the help of several of the bystanders, they lifted him out and unwrapped the tarpaulin, moving him on to a stretcher.

'We'd better get him to the ambulance and examine him there,' the leader of the team decided. Willing hands carried him up the beach with Nick and Madoc following. 'We'll take it from here,' they said politely. 'We'll check him over and then get him straight to Truro. Think he looks as if he'll be OK without calling the air ambulance. It's been quite a day for accidents with a major incident on the roads. But, I guess you won't have heard about that. Multiple pile up following a caravan blowing over. We've all been pretty stretched.' They were working as they chatted and soon had Anthony strapped to a stretcher with oxygen being supplied. OK, we'll be on our way now.'

'Thanks. Thanks very much,' Nick called as they shut the doors of the ambulance. The crowd around them were all asking what had happened and briefly, Madoc explained.

'It was all down to Nicola's superb skills as a sailor that we made it this far. Though he was unconscious for some of the time, I suspect his injuries are largely superficial. They'll probably keep him in for observation for a while. Now, I suppose we have to get this wretched boat back to the boatyard. We'd better give them a call and explain why we're so very late getting back.'

'Maybe they'll come and fetch it. I don't know about you but I'm exhausted and the weather's really turning quite stormy.' Her words were underlined as there was a clap of thunder. Rain began to fall, slowly at first and turning to large heavy drops in seconds. The crowd disappeared immediately and Nick and Madoc ran for cover up the beach. They were already soaked through and the rest of their belongings were left in the boat to get even wetter. 'Have you got a phone?' Nick asked. 'We need to call the boatyard right away.'

'Just hope it works after all this

damp,' Madoc grumbled. He had already put the boatyard number in the phone so he punched the buttons. Nick listened as he explained the problems. 'Of course it will cost us something. I don't care about that. We're both exhausted and the weather's foul. No way can we sail it back. No, it's not damaged at all. It's fine. We're at Porthaven. Yes, we can pull it up to the road . . . well, to the slipway. Yes. Fine. Thanks.'

He switched off. 'Honestly. You'd think they'd be pleased that we are being responsible. They have a call out charge of course. I don't care about that. Somehow, we have to get the boat up the beach to the slipway. Where have all these willing helpers gone? We could do with them now. Where did those guys in the boat disappear to? Don't know what we'd have done without them. I never thanked them properly.'

'I was too busy seeing Anthony into the ambulance. Shame, they deserved a thank you.'

As the rain was slowing down a little, they began to trudge down the soggy sand. Nick lowered the flapping sail and left it in the boat. They had no sail bag to stow it but it was far too wet in any case. They began the long haul up the beach. It was extremely heavy work and they could scarcely manage it. One or two men appeared and helped and Nick gave a sigh of relief. They finally retrieved their belongings and tried to decide what to do next.

'We'll have to wait for them to come with the trailer and maybe get a taxi back to the boatyard. Or perhaps they will be able to give us a lift in their van or whatever they bring.'

It was almost eight o'clock when they finally got back to their homes again. They even managed a wry laugh about their relaxing day.

'I don't care what you say but I'm taking you out for a decent meal after all this. Get yourself a shower and change of clothes and I'll pick you up in twenty minutes. No argument. Do it.'

'But . . . OK. Twenty minutes you said? No problem. Are you thinking of the pub?'

'That's right. It may be busy as it's Saturday but we both need a proper meal and time to unwind.'

★ ★ ★

The pub was indeed busy, but there was a corner table free in the dining room. Other diners were leaving and so the noise was gradually lessening. Madoc had decided it was time to talk and was waiting until they were served with their main courses. Nick spoke first.

'I was very impressed with your ingenuity today. The way you organised poor Anthony on his board and got it into the boat . . . well it was amazing.'

'I thought you were pretty amazing too. I totally panicked when we were sailing during the morning. If you hadn't taken over, I don't know how I'd have coped.'

'Next time, I'll give you some pointers if you like.'

'Next time? I doubt I'll ever set foot in a boat again.'

'I decided I'm definitely going to buy a dinghy so you'll have to come out again. I'll need a reliable crew.'

'But I was useless.'

'No you weren't. You achieved so much in a short time. And you did it to overcome a fear. That's impressive. We'll go out again soon in a hire craft and I'll look out for one of my own.'

'Can't say I'm that enthusiastic, all the same. But, OK. I'll come out as a crew with you, not as a helm. See, I'm getting the right terms, aren't I?'

Despite his intentions to talk to her, he was never quite able to bring himself to discuss his personal feelings and though it was a pleasant evening, he felt slightly dissatisfied at the end of it. Perhaps they were both a bit too exhausted for it anyway and it would be better discussed at a time when they were both more relaxed.

* * *

After all the drama of the previous day, Nick decided to have a quiet Sunday reading, pottering round the garden and doing odd jobs. She felt restored and on the Monday, Bank Holiday, she felt like doing something more interesting with her time. She wondered if Madoc might fancy a walk somewhere and decided to ring him. At the same time, her own phone rang. She was surprised to hear Paul's voice at the other end.

'How do you fancy a drive out to watch the surf competition at Fistral Beach? We can have lunch and then go on somewhere for the evening. I've got a day off from the lifeboat after the busy weekend. What do you think?'

'Well, thanks. Yes, I'd love to come. I was just wondering how to spend my day off. I've never watched a surf competition.'

'There's loads going on. Music. Concert etc. Plenty of stalls around too, so bring your purse. You might want to buy something. I'll pick you up in fifteen.'

'I don't mind driving if you . . . ' She paused. He had hung up. She just hoped it wouldn't be a day when he wanted to drink more than he should, when driving. She was turning into an old worry, she knew, but it was a law she felt strongly about. After working in an emergency unit at a hospital, traffic accidents had scared her and if drink was involved, she felt it was inexcusable.

She changed into her smartest jeans and a decent top and packed a bag with a towel, sun screen, a bottle of water and a fleece in case it turned cold later. She tucked in her phone and her wallet and was ready well before Paul turned up. Sorry Madoc, she said to the phone. I was just too late to call you. Again, Paul turned down her offer to drive. He was much too proud to allow anyone to drive him, especially a woman.

The beach was crowded when they arrived. Parking was a problem and he drew up at the side of the road, parking somewhat illegally.

'I'll be fine there. Only one wheel touching the yellow line. Nobody's going to bother today anyway. Right. Let's see what's going on.'

They watched the various competitors and finalists as they twisted and turned on their boards and made spectacular leaps to keep upright.

'Wow,' Nick said. 'I'd never be able to do that. Amazing control.' She couldn't understand how they scored points and why the winners actually won, but it had been fascinating to watch.

'Let's get something to eat. Fancy a hot dog?'

'Why not. Thanks. Actually, I'm sure it's my turn to pay.' They joined a long queue. How different from yesterday's healthy picnic, she thought, wondering what Madoc was doing today. He certainly wouldn't want to be here. Not his scene at all.

'I'll nip over to the beer tent and get some drinks, if you're sure. Mustard and relish on mine please. Meet you over there.' He pointed at a sign outside one of the tents and she nodded. When she had been served, she went to the appointed place and waited for Paul to turn up. He was ages. The hot dogs were cooling rapidly in the stiff breeze and she nibbled away at the edges of her own, wishing he would come soon.

'Sorry, love,' he said when he finally arrived carrying two pints of lager. 'I'm hopeless, aren't I? Never even asked what you'd like. If you don't drink lager, I'll just have to drink it for you.'

'I'll never manage a whole pint, but it's fine. Here, eat this while it's still slightly warm.' It wasn't the best she'd ever tasted but as she was hungry, she ate it anyway. The lager was slightly warm and not very pleasant either. Paul seemed not to notice and downed his quickly. When she said she'd had enough, he finished hers too. There was still a lot of the day to go and she began to worry about him driving them back. She grimaced slightly and decided to say nothing. If he drank more than she was comfortable with, like it or not, she would insist on getting a taxi back.

'Oh, so that's where you're hiding,' said one of a crowd who came out of the beer tent. 'Here, it's the one I owed you.' He handed Paul another pint of lager. 'Sorry love, I didn't get one for you. Didn't realise he was with anyone.'

'No worries,' Nick said automatically. What was she doing here? This was certainly not her scene and Paul didn't seem to be too bothered whether she was there or not.

'Now where did you manage to find this one?' the friend asked Paul. 'Very nice too.'

'Sorry, this is Nick. She was at our old school. One of the clever ones. Don't you remember her?'

'You know, I think I might. Long blonde pigtails and good at sports. He's too ignorant to introduce me, but I'm

Andy Parks. Same year as this repro-
bate.'

'Nice to meet you. Again, I suppose I
should say.'

'So what are you doing with yourself?
Why haven't we seen you around?'

Feeling somewhat bored, Nick explained.
Andy was making seriously flirty remarks
the whole time and every sentence was
filled with innuendo. She hated it. Could
she stick out a whole evening with this
crowd?

'I might go and look around some of
the stalls,' she told the group of noisy
men. They scarcely seemed to notice as
they laughed and joked. All lads
together, she thought with a grimace.

She wandered amongst the stalls, mostly
selling beach clothes, surf bits and pieces
and jewellery. Some things were nice
enough but she had lost interest in the
whole thing. She was tempted to walk
back into town and catch a bus back
home without saying anything. Perhaps
that was a bit rude and she needed to
let Paul know where she had gone.

She went back to the place she had left the group but they had all disappeared. Back into the beer tent no doubt. She looked inside and saw the heaving mass of humanity and made her decision. She would leave and find her own way back.

She found a piece of paper in her bag and wrote a note which she would put under the windscreen wipers on his car. That way he would stop looking for her once he was back at his car. This was all a big mistake. She and Paul had only one thing in common. Once upon a time, they had been to the same school. The kindness he had shown her on the lifeboat was his professional side. Away from that, he was not her sort of person at all. She'd had fun with him on the evenings out and sometimes, could feel as if she might be missing out on something in her life. Today had proved she was. But it was not Paul or his cronies. She went into town and caught a bus home.

Nick Hides Her Feelings For Madoc

Nick sat quietly that evening, contemplating her life. Today had at least proved some things to her. She was actually ready to settle down, not necessarily with another person or needing a big romance in her life but she needed to put down roots. If Madoc offered her a partnership, she could be happy to live here. But, he had had a number of opportunities, when Alan Lavers had finally agreed that he could no longer work and his partnership had become vacant. But Madoc had said nothing. Clearly he didn't have sufficient confidence in her abilities.

Her medical skills were not adequate for his needs. Though they seemed to get on well enough now, she presumed it must be the fact that he didn't want to work with a woman. This left her with one conclusion. She would have to leave this idyllic place and find herself another, permanent job. A job where she could progress and do things how she wanted to do them. She made up her mind to check out the medical magazines as soon as possible and see what vacancies there were. She had no attachments and would be free to move to anywhere that took her fancy.

When she arrived at the surgery the next morning, Nick went straight to the shelves of reference books and magazines. There were one or two that looked interesting but the application deadline was very close. She picked up the phone and left two messages for forms and details to be sent to her. Why didn't these people use the Internet and email? It was all so much quicker.

Madoc came in and looked at the magazines still open in front of her. He looked at her expectantly but she said nothing. She smiled and went into her room, taking one of the magazines with her. They hadn't spoken since Saturday's adventures and the meal afterwards. Nor had she heard anything from Paul. She hoped he hadn't drunk too much and had an accident. It was such an immature thing to do. As if on cue, her phone rang and she saw Paul's number come up.

'Hi,' she said, wondering what he was about to say. As she expected, he was angry.

'Nobody does that to me. Walking out on me was rude and quite unforgivable.'

'Actually, I did try to find you but you were so busy with your mates, you didn't notice me. Besides, you seemed to want to spend the time drinking with them so I felt unwanted and unwelcome. You're the one I'd call rude and unforgivable. I'm not one of your hang on the arm fashion accessories to be picked up and put down.'

'Whoa. I don't know what you think I am like. A few drinks with my mates does not mean you weren't with me for the day. I suppose I'm simply not clever enough to be with a fully fledged doctor as I believe you called yourself. Don't worry, love, I won't be bothering you again.' He put the phone down and she sat smiling cynically. He was most definitely not her type at all. Definitely the end of an era. There was a knock on her door and she called 'come in'.

'Just wondering if everything's all right?'

'Fine thanks. You?'

'I called round yesterday to see if you fancied a walk along the coast. Thought we might have tried driving somewhere and exploring a new area. But you were out.'

'Yes. Went out with a friend. Unexpected and a bit of a disaster but hey, that's life.'

'Can I ask why you're looking at the medical mags?'

'Job hunting. I think it's time I settled down and got a permanent job. I've been doing temporary things for long enough.'

'But I thought you were happy here? Thinking of buying a boat and staying around?' She looked at him long and hard without speaking. She was waiting for him to say something more. There was another knock on her door. Emma came in.

'Sorry to interrupt, but your patient's waiting, Nick. And yours is just coming in, Madoc.'

'Thanks. Send her in. We've finished our chat.'

'To be continued,' Madoc told her. 'Come to my place for supper this evening. We need to talk.'

She nodded her acceptance and tried hard to bring her brain back to the task in hand.

* * *

It was a busy day, with a number of people seeming to have been injured or unwell following the holiday weekend. Nick felt weary by the end of it and ready to be looked after that evening.

She felt sure that Madoc was about to tell her to leave once he had found someone more suitable to join the practice and was pleased she had begun to take her own steps towards moving on.

Slightly apprehensive, she opened the door to the surgery that evening and knocked at the kitchen door to Madoc's private area of the building. He had laid the table carefully and even lit candles. It seemed oddly out of character.

'This all looks very inviting,' she said carefully.

'Emma's idea. She said you might appreciate candles. Do sit down. I've got some white wine chilling. Hope that's all right?'

'Lovely. Thanks. Very thoughtful. Are you joining me?'

'As you know, I don't drink but there's no reason other people shouldn't enjoy a drink in moderation.' He poured a glass for her and sipped mineral water himself. He put out a plate of warm garlic bread. 'I've got some fresh bream baking in the oven. Hope you like it.'

'Love it, thanks.'

'Look, the reason I asked you here was to give us a chance to talk.'

'You said.'

'I don't want you to leave. Please re-consider and stay here. I know I always thought I couldn't work with a woman but you have made yourself indispensable. We seem to work well together and certainly complement each other in our particular skills. What do you say?'

'I . . . well I'm not sure. I really do love it here but I never feel you quite approve of me, medically I mean.'

'How can you think that? Don't I compliment you?'

'Occasionally, but usually it's outside work. Like on Saturday. You told me I was brilliant at sailing but never speak about my medical skills. And you've intimated that you want another male to replace Doctor Lavers.'

'I've never said that.' His dark eyes flashed angrily. What was it with this woman? He thought he had let her know he was pleased with the way things had gone. Were going. He pushed his hair from his face and it promptly fell back. Nick longed to push it away herself and feel the soft curls. She realised she actually longed to be held by him but there was a huge wall between them.

Emma had been right that first day. He was rather a rugged hero type, despite his failings. 'I'd like you to stay on. Please don't consider leaving.' The timer on the oven pinged and he got up to rescue their meal. He took a bowl of salad from the fridge and jacket potatoes from the oven. The fish was perfectly cooked in foil wrapped packets, with a butter and herb sauce.

'Wow, feed me like this and you're on.'

'Please be serious, Nicola. Will you stay here and work with me?'

'Let's not spoil this wonderful meal with talking. Save it till we've eaten. Besides, I need to think about it properly.' They ate almost in silence.

'That was wonderful. Thank you.' He poured her another glass of wine. She spoke again. 'I had convinced myself that I need to move on. That there isn't a future for me here. Especially with you. We seem to get on well but I never feel I have got any closer to the real Madoc Roskelly. The man behind the doctor's exterior.'

'I assumed Emma had told you about my history. She's an excellent secretary and usually very discreet but I am sure she wouldn't have resisted telling you that I've become such a misogynist because of my dreadful marriage.'

'Well, yes. She did give me the brief gist of it.'

'My wife was a very beautiful woman and I was flattered at being targeted by her. We were married in Exeter where I was working at the hospital. She wanted to be a respectable doctor's wife and hoped I was going to become a high-powered surgeon or consultant. When she discovered I expected her to live here with me and be a humble GP's wife, she hated every minute of it. I came back to work with my father for a while before he retired.

'She did come here with me, rather grudgingly but she was bored silly. She kept arranging parties and organising large dinners with friends in expensive restaurants, assuming I'd pick up the bills all the time. Her parents had stables and kept her horse there. She went up to stay with them to go hunting whenever she could. I abhor hunting and tried to get her to give it up. Naturally, she thought having affairs with any man that came her way, was all perfectly acceptable. My patients began to make remarks and it was all affecting my work.

'I decided she had to go and she dragged it all out as long as possible, trying to ruin my good name in the process. Eventually we were divorced and it all served to make me distrust all women. I've vaguely tried to have another relationship from time to time but it was hopeless. I thought I may be getting towards acceptance by you but now you say you want to leave.'

'Only because you have never asked me to stay.'

'I want you to stay. I've become very fond of you, Nicola. I could even grow to love you . . . if I dared. But you have shown you have other friends who would give you a more interesting, livelier time. You're younger than me and probably need to go out to these nightclubs and things.'

'You really don't know me very well at all, do you? Yes I've been out with someone a few times but there's really nothing to it. I only went for a change of routine and in fact, that's all over now anyway. After a disastrous time yesterday, I certainly won't be seeing Paul again.'

'He's the sports car, I gather?' She nodded. 'And there's nobody else on the scene?'

'Nobody.'

'And what about us? Could you ever

see a future for us? Assuming you did stay here?'

'I'm not sure. There are still some problems, I fear. Let me think about one thing at a time.'

He grimaced slightly assuming this was a brush off. How could he hope to have any success with someone like her?

'There's some ice-cream if you'd like some. I didn't have time to make anything exotic.'

'Ice-cream would be lovely. Thank you.' She frowned as he left the table to get it. What exactly was he saying? He wanted her to stay but did he mean the future included a relationship or simply a working relationship? How could she possibly have a future with someone who never wanted to have a family? He had said he might grow to love her. That wasn't exactly flattering. If she stayed here, he might get used to her, enough to love her? Not much of a compliment.

★ ★ ★

At the end of the evening, she thanked him for the meal. He took her arm and pulled her close to him. She could feel his heart beating against her own. He bent to kiss her and she felt herself seeming to float away. She felt him trembling against her and then suddenly, he pulled away again.

'I'm sorry, Nicola. So sorry.' He opened the door and whispered goodnight.

'Thank you again for the meal. It was lovely. And thank you for telling me about yourself. It explains a lot.' With her knees feeling quite weak, she walked down the hill to her cottage.

Inside, she slumped down on to the sofa. Her mind was in a whirl, not to mention her body. He had kissed her as if he meant it and then apologised. Why? What was he actually apologising for? Kissing her in the first place? Or maybe he didn't think he'd done it properly? It was all too confusing. Disturbing, even. She knew perfectly well that she could very easily fall in love with this man. His kiss had awoken feelings in her that she had pushed aside for many years. Since college days, in fact. But it was all pointless. She had to find another job but this time, she would look for something permanent and somewhere she really wanted to make her home. But would stay here for as long as it took to find her ideal placement.

★ ★ ★

Nick and Madoc both found it difficult the next morning. They were polite to each other to what seemed a ridiculous degree, each tiptoeing round each other and avoiding speaking more than the absolute minimum. He left to take his clinic in the other village.

Two large envelopes were waiting on her desk. Madoc must have brought in the mail and left them for her. They were the application forms and information about the jobs she had looked at the previous day. She tightened her lips and ripped open the envelopes. Both looked quite interesting but she really didn't want to work in city centre practices. She must stick to her decision and wait till the right job came up.

She put the forms back in the envelopes and put them to one side and went into the reception area. Emma was sitting in front of her computer, looking positively grey in the face and clutching her chest.

'Emma?' she called anxiously. 'Emma? What's the matter?'

'Can't breathe,' she gasped. 'Hurts.' She pointed at her chest. 'And here.' She indicated her left jaw line. Nick grabbed her stethoscope and listened. She felt Emma's forehead.

'Just sit quietly for a minute or two. Try to breathe slowly and steadily.' She gave the secretary a low dose aspirin and a drink of water and then took her blood pressure. It was very high.

'What is it?' Emma asked as her colour was coming back and her breathing improved. 'It isn't my heart is it?'

'I think you may be showing symptoms of angina. We need to do some tests and get you sorted. Hopefully, we can start you on some medication which will control it but we need to be sure that's all it is. I'm going to send off some bloods and I'll see if we can get you in immediately for more tests. I'll give you a spray to use if you ever have another attack like that one.'

'But my work. I need to sort out the patients and appointments and . . . oh dear.' Tears filled her eyes and she slumped forward, her head on her hands. 'I've been dreading something like this. I just don't know what Derek will say. He'll never manage.'

'Hey, come on now. It may not be as bad as you fear. Let's get a diagnosis before we panic. Just sit there quietly. No, better still, go and sit in my room. That way you won't have to deal with patients coming in.'

'But who's going to deal with them?'

'It'll be fine. Come on now. I'll help you through.' Once Emma was settled, Nick phoned the hospital and explained the situation. They made an urgent appointment for her to be seen the next morning. Meanwhile, she needed to go home and rest. Somehow, they would have to manage without her. It would have to be Madoc's morning to take the outreach clinic. She would have to phone him and let him know about the problems and she needed to get Emma home. She quickly wrote a notice for the door and taped it outside.

Due to an emergency, appointments will be approximately 30 minutes late. Apologies for the inconvenience.

'Come on now, Emma. I'm taking you home.' The secretary opened her mouth to argue but Nick hushed her. 'Where's Derek today? Can I get hold of him?' She had learned that Derek had a gardening round and worked in several different gardens both in this village and the next one. 'Does he have a mobile phone with him?'

'Oh dear, I don't like to bother him. And I'll be all right walking home. I feel better now.' Nick ignored her and bundled her into the car, carefully locking the surgery door behind them. Luckily, she had driven her car up the hill this morning as she had planned to go straight out to make house calls after morning appointments. She wasn't entirely sure how they were going to manage. Drat, she realised, she had forgotten to switch on the answering machine. She would have to get Emma settled and return as quickly as possible.

When she returned, there were several people waiting. They were all good humoured and wanted to know what the problem was. It would soon be all round the village anyway, so she simply told them that Emma was unwell and had gone home. There were rumours of she hasn't looked well lately and she never has anything wrong.

'Give me a few moments and I'll see you soon,' Nick told them. She would have to trust them to leave things alone in the waiting area. She went into her room and phoned Madoc.

'Oh heavens, how on earth are we going to manage? I've got full house here today, as well.'

'I'll do what I can. Might not manage the house calls. I'll put the answering machine on to field the phone calls but I'll have to leave the place unattended. I suppose Auntie Dolly couldn't come in?'

'Don't you dare. She'll have everyone taking her weird concoctions in a matter of minutes. I'll think of something.'

It was certainly not the best of mornings. She had to hurry her patients and was unable to give them the usual time. Every now and then, she needed to go and see to the phone. There were a number of calls that needed urgent attention and that slowed down her consultations even more.

Luckily, people were mostly good humoured about it, apart from the occasional person who was in a hurry. Nick had to pile the patient records into a box to be sorted out later once they had been seen. It was going to be chaos if they didn't get something organised promptly. Her last patient was finally admitted. It was Mrs Clarkson from the pharmacy.

'I don't know if it would help, but my daughter's still home on holiday before she goes to college. She doesn't go for a couple of weeks and she's quite good on the phone and can use a computer. If Doctor Roskelly wants her, I'm sure she'd be pleased to earn a few pounds and help you out. He does know our Maddy.'

'Well thanks. I'll certainly tell him. Now, is there something I can do for you?'

It was way past lunch time when she had finally caught up on the office side of things. Madoc came back and wanted her to catch up on everything that had happened. She mentioned Maddy Clarkson and he pulled a face.

'Nice enough girl but I'm not sure how discreet she can be. She's rather young for the responsibility. But I guess needs must.'

'So, what do you think is wrong with Emma?'

'I'm almost certain it's angina. Her blood pressure is high and she has all the classic symptoms. I've got her an appointment for an ECG tomorrow. Shame we haven't got a machine here. Don't think they're too expensive. It would save a lot of time and stress. Anyway, I've taken bloods as well and asked for an urgent diagnosis. Thought I'd call round to see her later and maybe start her on some blood pressure reducing pills.'

'She never struck me as a possible heart disease patient. She's underweight if anything, doesn't smoke and walks to work every day so we know she has exercise. One of these cases where the genes influence it all. Honestly, of all the times for this to happen.'

'What do you mean?'

'We're still pretty busy, despite the end of the holiday season. This is when the older folks come for their holidays and we sometimes get busier than ever.'

'The poor woman didn't get ill on purpose you know.'

'Of course not. But it's very inconvenient and I just don't see how we'll manage. You're not entirely up to speed with the system are you?'

'Madoc, what on earth are you saying? Last night I was just what you need to keep the practice going. Now you're telling me I can't cope. Poor Emma is ill. I don't know how she's put up with you all these years. She deserves better.'

'Hmm. Well, yes, I admit she's ill and deserves sympathy but we're doing what we can for the woman. You're positively nurse-maiding her. Can't get better than that.'

'So, what do we do about Maddy Clarkson?'

'I suppose we'd better see her and if

she's any good, take her on for a while. We clearly can't manage without any receptionist or secretary. I'll give Mrs C a call.'

Nick set off on her rounds, somewhat belatedly and had to make her visits brief. Luckily there was nothing serious, the usual round of high temperatures and assorted infections. Madoc's harsh words still rankled with her. It was almost time for evening surgery by the time she was back in the office with a string of scribbled notes in Madoc's illegible handwriting. Seemed he'd had a busy afternoon.

There was one more cheerful bit of news. He'd seen Maddy and she was coming in the next morning. That was some relief. Fortunately, it was a light surgery with fewer patients than usual but by six o'clock, Nick was visibly wilting. She'd had nothing to eat for lunch except an apple she had been invited to pick from the tree in the garden of one of her patients.

All she wanted to do now was to go

home, have a shower and heat up something in the microwave. Then she might slump in front of something light hearted on the television. Madoc stopped her as she was leaving.

'Thanks for all your efforts today,' he said. 'You managed very well this morning in an emergency.'

'Thanks,' she said slightly surprised.

'I'm trying to make sure I let you know I appreciate you,' he said with a wry grin. 'I'm sorry about this morning. I was unfair. Erm . . . I was wondering . . . have you thought any more about our discussion last night?'

'When exactly have I had time to think about anything? I'm tired and I haven't eaten all day. Don't try to pressure me. I will think about it. About us. But you do give out such mixed messages. I am confused and I don't really know where we stand.'

'Come and have dinner with me at the pub. We can talk there.'

'Not tonight, Madoc. But thank you. I need to unwind and relax and I want my own company for once. Time to think, even?'

'Fair enough. Have a pleasant evening.'

'You know, it might do you good to have a glass or two of wine and relax a bit. Can work wonders you know.'

'You know nothing,' he snapped. 'Good night.' He turned back into his own room with an expression that reminded Nick of a child with a favourite toy that had just broken. She desperately wanted to fling her arms round him and tell him everything would be all right. But she didn't know if it would, did she?

★ ★ ★

She fell asleep almost as soon as she had finished eating. The television blared on without her.

'Goodness,' she said aloud when she awoke at ten-thirty. 'I've turned into my parents.' They regularly slept through most television programmes, even the ones they really wanted to watch.

* ★ ★ ★

Maddy arrived promptly the next morning and Madoc ran through her duties with her. He said repeatedly that he expected her to be totally discreet and never mention anything outside these walls. She assured him she knew what was expected and seemed to understand perfectly about the appointment system and sorting out patient notes.

'I'm afraid I had to leave yesterday's notes out and they need filing. Can you manage that do you think?' Nick asked the girl. She was a pretty girl, dressed in rather bright colours and seemed to have a mass of things hanging round her neck. Beads, a shiny scarf with long ends that dangled almost to the floor and a mass of hair the colour of an Irish Setter Nick's family had once owned. It was a glorious shade but not at all natural with the rest of her colouring.

Long pendant earrings dangled from her ears, looking as if they might all get tangled together if she shook her head. She didn't exactly look like a medical receptionist but maybe she would manage. Nick felt uncertain about the new addition.

'Right, well you know where I am if you need any help. Just don't come in when a patient is with me.'

'Okey dokey,' Maddy said brightly and rather too loudly. 'What time's coffee break?'

'When we have time, usually at the end of surgery.'

The girl grimaced. 'If I last that long. Joke,' she added when Madoc's expression darkened. He raised an eyebrow towards Nick and she gave a shrug.

The morning seemed to go reasonably smoothly and things looked organised by the time surgery was over. Maddy assured them that she was in control so they both relaxed. Nick was having the rest of the day off until evening surgery, while Madoc made house calls. She planned to see Emma and find out how the tests had gone.

She was hoping that the receptionist's condition could be managed with medication and that she would not require surgery.

She logged on to the internet and managed to get Emma's blood test results from the hospital. She certainly needed statins, medication to reduce her cholesterol level. She quickly went through to see Madoc and discuss the options. He agreed with Nick's diagnosis and she wrote out a prescription, planning to call at the pharmacy on her way round to Emma's house.

'If we can't look after her properly, we'll be making our own lives more difficult,' she laughed when Madoc had said rather too politely that it was very kind of her to take such trouble.

★   ★   ★

Emma was most grateful for Nick's attention and said she felt better already. She had taken her reliever spray once yesterday and seemed to have been all right this morning. Derek had taken time off work to be with her at the hospital and now he had gone to try to catch up.

'I've brought you some pills to take and there are a couple of booklets for you to read. Nothing too scary and we'll hope this is all the treatment you'll need. You may have to have an angiogram to make a proper diagnosis but we'll talk about that later when we get more results. We've got Maddy Clarkson coming in to man the phone and make appointments.'

'She's a bit of an airhead that one. Don't know how she ever got into university. Still if it means you can manage without me, I'll be able to relax a bit. Thanks Nick. You've been very kind.'

Nick decided she needed to relax herself and drove to one of the local beaches, away from Gwillian, so she didn't meet too many of her patients. There were a few people around and she sat on a rock, staring out to sea.

Something hypnotic and calming about watching the waves breaking on the shore, she was thinking, before her mind turned to what she really needed to consider.

Maybe she should go home to her parents for the weekend, talk things through with them and get away from the closeness of the village and people. Separating the relationship side and professional side of this medical practice was a difficult one. In many ways, this was her ideal job. A small enough practice to get to know her patients with scope to improve their service. But she needed to sort out her emotions and decide if she really could work with Madoc and even if they might have any sort of future together.

Madoc Feels He's Losing Nick

The next few days gave both doctors some concern. Patients records were getting rather muddled and several times, patients had arrived for appointments without the doctors being informed. Madoc was finding it difficult to cope and lost his temper a couple of times. The crisis came when Nick had been in the village shop buying her vegetables. Maggie Fletcher said how sorry she was to hear that one of the younger girls in the village was suffering from scabies.

'It's shocking. And to think that madam was trying to persuade Tommy to go out with her. I just hope he wasn't flattered by the attention. She's such a pretty girl, I have to admit. What a dreadful worry for her parents. Not that they're the best of course.'

'I'm sorry, Maggie, but I really don't know what you're talking about.'

'That Willis girl. You know, the elder one. Always looks like being trouble, that one with looks like that.'

'I don't know what you think is going on, Maggie, but I know nothing. Even if I did it would be a case of breaching medical confidentiality if I commented. I really don't want to hear this sort of gossip. In fact, I don't even know how such things get around.'

'Fine. I'll say nothing more. But I know it's true. Came from a reliable source.'

'Nick was fuming when she came out of the shop. She hated gossip at the best of times and if there was one thing she disliked about this place it was the fact that everyone seemed to know everyone's business. She dropped off her shopping and went straight to the surgery. Maddy was talking on the phone, clearly to one of her friends as she quickly stopped laughing and changed the subject as she saw Nick arriving.'

'Very well, I'll make a note of it,' she said and put the phone down. 'Oh, hello, Nick. I didn't think you were in this morning.'

'Just a few things I need to check on. I need to look at some patients notes.'

'Oh, righty-o. Who is it? I'll find them for you.'

'No, it's fine. I'll get them myself.' She turned her back on the girl and looked through to find the Willis family notes. Sally, Fiona, Alistair, Joan. Which was the elder daughter? She collected them all and took them into her room. It was Fiona. She scanned through the notes. She was one of Madoc's patients and indeed, she did have scabies. Now how on earth had that information got out?

As it happened, things moved on before she had the opportunity. Madoc was finishing his own surgery when there was an upset in the reception area. She heard shouting and angry voices and went to see what was happening. Madoc came out of his room, furious at the racket.

'What's going on here?' he demanded with one of his leonine roars.

'Sorry, it's Mrs Willis and her daughter,' Maddy announced. 'They wanted to see you immediately. I said you were with someone and they'd have to wait. Then she started kicking off. Didn't like it.'

'I see. If you can give me a moment. I'll finish with my patient and then I'll see you.'

'It isn't right. Discussing things. I've got a good mind to sue the lot of you.'

'Please, Mrs Willis. Perhaps you can go into Doctor Quenby's room with her. I'll join you as soon as I finish.'

Nick led the woman and her daughter into her own room, hastily pushing into a drawer the patients' notes she had been looking at. Their notes.

'Please have a seat. Doctor Roskelly shouldn't be long.'

At last, Madoc arrived and Nick breathed a sigh of relief.

'What I want to know, Doctor, is how comes half the village knows about my daughter and her illness?'

'I really have no idea what you're talking about. We have the strictest rules about patient confidentiality. If the news has become the subject of gossip then I am sorry but I doubt it has come from this practice. Are you sure Fiona herself hasn't said something?'

'Course she hasn't.'

'There are only the two of us and Mrs Liddicoat who have access to patient notes. They are kept locked in filing cabinets the rest of the time. I can assure you of our complete discretion.'

'And that Maddy out there. Does she have access to the files?'

'Well, yes.' He paused, suddenly struck with horror. 'Maddy assured me she understood about the need for privacy. I assure you I will certainly follow this up.'

'Fetch her in here now. I want answers.'

'I will let you know, Mrs Willis. I'm not prepared to have some sort of shouting match in this room. Now, if you don't mind leaving, I will inform you of the results of my inquiry.'

'You'd better. I won't let this rest, mark my word. I'll sue if necessary.'

'Nicola, would you ask Maddy to step in here please?'

Looking scared, Maddy sidled into the room and stood on one side of the desk.

'Can you explain how this rumour got out? About Fiona Willis?'

Maddy went scarlet and hung her head. 'Come on. Clearly you know exactly what I'm talking about it's also perfectly obvious that you know so don't try to pretend you don't.'

'I couldn't help seeing what was in her notes.'

'Even so, it was not for you to make comment, was it? You've probably caused this practice a whole lot of trouble.' Madoc was doing his best to control himself but Nick didn't miss the tightening of his mouth.

'My mum'll kill me if I lose this job,' she said in a choked voice.

'You still broke the rules. Rules that are really set in stone. You're very young. I hope you'll learn from this. Good job you've already got your uni place or this could have really messed things up.'

'I'm really sorry. Really I am. I'd never do anything like this again. Do you think Doctor Roskelly might re-consider?'

'No chance.' Nick was adamant. 'Just get yourself away and out of sight.'

Nick felt unable to speak and glared as she went back into Madoc's room.

'Somehow, we've now got to manage until Emma's well enough to return to work. It'll mean a lot more work for us but it's the only way I can see until we know more. We'll record a new message in the answering machine and just have to allow more time each day to call people back with appointments. I'll have to do the filing during the evening,' Madoc said.

'Maybe we could get an agency receptionist. There must be someone who can help us.'

'This is Cornwall, not Bristol or somewhere with masses of people with the sort of skills that we need. I'm not willing to risk anything like this happening again.'

The next few days were something of a nightmare. Whenever either of them was trying to use the filing cabinet, the computer or the phone, the other was already there. Nick had managed to call on Emma a couple of times and not let on about the current chaos. She was feeling much better and wanting to come back to work.

Nick wouldn't listen and told her to rest a while longer. If nothing else, she wanted to make sure everything was tidy and up to date before Emma came back to the sort of muddle they were living in at present.

By Friday, Madoc was in a bad temper most of the time. Even his favourites at The Beeches were getting short shrift and Nick felt ready to walk out at any moment. She had decided against going to see her parents at the weekend, knowing that she needed to stay and try to catch up on the work scene. No more mention of the future had been uttered and both doctors were fighting hard to keep things moving.

Auntie Dolly had arrived on a couple of occasions, bringing one of her herbal teas to help them relax. She offered to help by answering the phone but on the one occasion she had done so, when they were both out of the room briefly, she had told the patient they should not be bothering the overworked doctors, unless it was a dire emergency. Nobody discovered if it was ever truly an emergency of any sort. Auntie Dolly was not receptionist material.

'How are you getting on with my boy?' she had asked Nick just as she was leaving.

'All right, thanks.'

'You getting things together then?'

'I'm not sure.'

'So you don't know if you'll be staying on? I need to take steps,' she said once again, 'Just to make certain of things.'

'I'm sure I don't know what you mean, Auntie Dolly,' Nick said anxiously. 'I'm still thinking things through.'

Auntie Dolly peered at her with those dark eyes. Nick felt as if she were looking straight through her and into her darkest depths. Exactly what could she find there? Maybe it was little more than a seething mass of scattered thoughts.

* * *

On Saturday morning, Nick strolled up the hill and let herself into the reception area. She went behind the desk and unlocked the filing cabinet, ready to begin sorting the bundle of notes she had left in there the previous day. They had gone, all neatly filed away in their proper places. Madoc must have done it. She went into her own room, taking the appointment book with her. At least she could familiarise herself with some of the cases that she needed to see and follow through. She heard someone outside her door and got up to check that it was Madoc.

'What are you doing here on a Saturday?' he asked.

'I came to file the records. I left things in a muddle last night.'

'I sorted it. I was doing my own anyhow so it didn't take long to do the rest. I'm now going to work on the practice accounts.'

'How about I give you a hand and then we go out for a walk. It's a gorgeous morning.'

'Pub lunch at Trevast?'

She nodded. 'OK, you're on. It's a fairly simple matter of putting in figures and balancing a couple of columns. In theory that is.'

'It's been quite a week.'

'Sorry if I've been impossible. It's the usual way when things go badly wrong.'

'I've been pretty grumpy too. Come on then, let's get this job done and we can enjoy what's left of the day. We've both been working too hard.'

'Do you think Emma might be back on Monday?'

'Certainly, if I say we need her, she'll be in like a shot. I still don't know if the consultant is recommending an angiogram.'

They worked companionably for an hour and managed to complete their task. She went to her cottage to change into walking boots, and they set off along the cliff tops. There was a stiff breeze blowing but the sky was a clear blue and the sea matched the colour, with white foamy trimmings at the base of the cliffs and rocks.

'We work well together when we try, don't we?' Nick said.

'I suppose. I'd never have believe it would turn out quite so well.'

'Nor did I on that first morning. I

very nearly turned round and left you to it. But apart from the odd disagreement, we've survived nearly four months.'

'Have you had time to think any more about staying or not?'

'I'd really like to, but I am determined that my next placement is going to be a permanent one. It's time I put down roots.'

'Does that mean in your personal life as well?'

She frowned as she pondered the question.

'Maybe. But I need to sort my career first of all. I see opportunities here. There are so many things we could improve and add to the practice and I'd love to be able to do that. But I'm not getting any younger. Oh how I hate that silly phrase, but it's appropriate.'

'So, is there anyone on the scene who might make you stay?'

'Possibly. Just vaguely possibly,' she said enigmatically. She knew she was more than fond of this man with all his faults and failings but there remained the one huge problem. Children. Was it such a huge thing in reality or was it just something she had always dreamed about? With a fulfilling career and a potentially loving husband, did she really need more? As ever, the answer was a resounding yes. She did want a family and as she was almost twenty-nine, she needed to be thinking more about her own needs and future.

'Round the next corner I believe. I shall be ready for a drink. We should have brought some water with us.'

They sat outside the pub and watched the activity on the little beach. One or two children were playing the endless games of building dykes and trying to stop the tide from destroying it.

'I never really did that sort of thing when I was a kid. I quickly felt bored with the beach sort of stuff. Couldn't see much point in digging like mad for nothing and seeing it washed away. As there was only me, I never played ball games or any of these other things the kids do. Dad was always busy and Mum too, I guess.'

'Sounds a bit of a lonely existence.'

'I s'pose it was but I didn't know anything different. There weren't many kids around and they all seemed a bit rough and tumble. I went to boarding school from about ten years old so never got to know the local kids at all.'

'I love the beach. Couldn't get enough of it. My sister and I used to play together quite well for sisters, I suppose. And her two kids love it too.' She reminisced about childhood holidays. It served to make her even more certain that she would never be content without a family of her own.

The drinks were brought out to them, along with cutlery for their meal. She had opted for a large glass of shandy and he was drinking his usual mineral water.

'Don't you get sick of it?' Nick asked.

'What, water? No, I often have other things too.'

'What puts you off drinking alcohol? Have you never even tried it?'

'At medical school I did. But I wasn't keen.'

'Very strange. Surely in moderation it's all right? I mean, I enjoy wine but I don't drink vast quantities.'

'If you must know, my father was an alcoholic.'

'What, the lovely Doctor Roskelly my parents were so fond of?'

'The very same. He hid it well. My mother didn't realise for many years but when he started hiding bottles in all sorts of odd places, she became suspicious. He collapsed at one point and couldn't do his job. He went off for treatment and I took over the practice with Alan Lavers and when Dad returned, he had decided to retire to the holiday home they had bought years before. Fortunately, he's been able to stay off alcohol and they now have a good life in Spain. It served to put me off forever.'

'I see. Thanks for telling me. Promise

I won't ask why you're not drinking ever again.'

'I trust you'll keep this to yourself?'

'Of course. I'd never tell anyone. Does Emma know? And Auntie Dolly?'

'I think they both suspected but didn't know for sure. Ah, lunch at last.'

They ate hungrily and soon cleared their plates. The children on the beach had drifted away and several youngsters had arrived with surf boards. The waves looked enticing and Nick almost wished she could join them. Madoc was watching her face.

'You'd like to be out there with them, wouldn't you, Nicola?'

'I guess. We're poles apart, aren't we?'

'In some ways. But don't let it put you off completely. Please. We do work well together. Your ability with children and mine with the older folk are good. You know why I'm so scared to ever contemplate having children?'

'Not really. Tell me.'

'My ex-wife decided she wanted

children when the time was right. I told her of my worries about being a hopeless father but she said it would all be fine when I had a child of my own. She intended to employ a nanny and have someone to come and clean and even have a cook. She said she couldn't possibly be expected to do everything for a child. I said we wouldn't be able to afford it, especially if she was intent on all her entertaining. Her answer to that was that 'Daddy would help out'.'

'She also intended asking him to buy us a decent house. I felt totally emasculated. As if I couldn't provide for my own wife. Besides, I didn't want us to have children, I'd already decided that we weren't going to have a happy marriage by then. Add children to the mix, it would be a disaster for me and them. Clearly she only wanted them because it proved something to the world. Little dolls she could dress up and parade around her friends. Horrible. I've never actually known any small children, except the ones that come to the surgery when they're not well. They just seem to yell all the time. And it's the parents who really need help, rarely the children.'

'Wow. Thanks for explaining it all to me. You certainly do have a complex about it. I'll go and pay for lunch. It's my turn.' He was about to protest but instead, said thanks. He wasn't used to an independent female.

'Shall we walk back then?' she said as she returned to their table.

He stared at her and gave a shrug. He felt he was losing her and he didn't know how to stop it happening. The silence between them was palpable. It was no longer a companionable silence with one or other of them occasionally pointing out various sea birds or flowers and plants.

Nick was busy with her own thoughts with strings of questions buzzing through her mind. Could she work closely with Madoc, potentially fall in love with him but knowing all the time it could never work? Could she manage to have a relationship with no possibility of a family? How could she give up this wonderful place? In so many ways, this was where she wanted to be. She looked at the man striding out beside her. He was so solid and dependable. He was a good doctor and they shared many interests. She wondered what he was thinking.

Madoc's brain was also busy. He kept giving surreptitious glances at the girl beside him. She was so beautiful with her clear blue eyes and pretty blonde hair. She was slim, not too slim but perfectly shaped in his mind. She was active and lively and seemed to share his thoughts on so many things. He saw a peregrine falcon take off in front of them and would normally have commented but did not want to interrupt her thoughts. She looked as if she was miles away and he felt the gulf between them widen.

With a happy childhood like hers behind her, it was obvious she would want a family of her own. But how, if she would even consider him as a potential partner, would he cope with babies?

He felt uncomfortable in the presence of children and young babies were something he'd really prefer not to encounter at all. But for Nicola, might he be able to stifle his dislike? Would it not be worth it? He gave a shudder and hoped she hadn't noticed.

Gwillian was in sight. It was such a pretty village, tucked into its own little bay. A small harbour and stretch of sand with a clutch of pretty old cottages on the narrow lanes leading down to the sea made it an idyllic Cornish setting. The larger, modern estates were high above the village out of sight of the picturesque part of the village.

'Do you want a cup of tea?' Nick asked as they reached her cottage.

'If you've got time. Thanks.' He hesitated, wondering if this was the right time to speak his thoughts. Fearing her answer would not be the one he wanted, he decided to leave it until she spoke of her own accord. They sat quietly sipping tea in her tiny garden. It was still sunny and warm, typical of September in Cornwall.

'I should do some weeding,' she said. 'The borders are getting rather over-grown.'

'I'll give you a hand, if you like. I find gardening quite relaxing whenever I get round to doing any. Doesn't Auntie Dolly have someone coming in to do it, though?'

'Not since I've been here. Maybe she does when there are just holiday makers coming for short stays.'

'I'd better go,' Madoc decided. 'I'll certainly come and help you with some gardening. Tomorrow maybe?' He felt the conversation was getting polite and stilted and thought she might have seen enough of him for one day.

'If you like. I haven't any plans. I had planned to go and see my parents this weekend but when we had the Maddy crisis, I thought I'd better stay and get things more organised.'

'Sorry. I hadn't realised. OK then, I'll come down about ten tomorrow?'

'Thanks. That's kind of you.'

Nick sat out in the garden for another half an hour. She had wondered whether to go to the beach with her surfboard but thought Paul might be there. She didn't want another encounter with him after his unpleasantness. Besides, she felt weary after the long walk and decided to take it easy. She wandered down to the village shop and browsed through the DVDs they were renting out. She picked up a couple of films she had missed seeing and with a bottle of wine, prepared for an indulgent, lazy evening. She needed to take her mind off her future and stop her thoughts going round and round.

★   ★   ★

When she awoke on Sunday morning, the rain was falling heavily. After yesterday's glorious weather, it was most unexpected. Madoc rang at nine-thirty and said there was no point attempting any work outside so he planned to do some sorting in his office.

'Do you want me to help?' Nick offered.

'No, it's fine. You relax and get yourself ready for another week of exceptionally hard work. See you in the morning.'

She was bored. All the things she wanted to do at this moment relied on good weather. She rang her mother and discovered that she was in the middle of cooking Sunday lunch for her sister and her family. She felt isolated and a bit left out. It was entirely her own fault and if she hadn't stayed here for the weekend she would have been a part of it.

'You could always come up darling,' her mother invited. 'There's plenty of food and it's ages since we saw you. I can delay serving till you get here. It's less than a couple of hours drive.'

'I'd love to, Mum, but then it's

another two hours home again afterwards. We've got a bit of a situation at work and I'm working all hours at present. Otherwise, I'd have been home this weekend for sure.'

'Let me call you back later and we'll talk about it. You are all right, aren't you? I mean there's nothing seriously wrong? You're not ill or anything?'

'Course not, Mum. I'm fine. Bit stressed and overworked but I'm fine. Speak again soon. Love to everyone. Bye.'

She wondered what Madoc was doing but decided against going there. She sat down with her laptop and decided to look at the medical vacancies site. If there was something there that appealed, it might make her decision for her. In any case, she could always take yet another temporary locum post until the perfect job came up. There was nothing that appealed but she realised that simply by looking, she had reached a decision. She would speak to Madoc at the first opportunity.

Auntie Dolly's Love Potions May Work

The week began as busily as the doctors had expected. The appointment system was becoming chaotic with queues of patients seeming to turn up at the wrong times or all at the same time. Nick was feeling totally exhausted by the end of the second day.

Madoc was doing his best to take the load away from her as much as he could and was himself working late into each evening. He was writing the referral letters himself, filing notes and generally covering all of Emma's work and some of Nick's as well. He sensed that she had made her decision to leave and was doing his best to make her think it wasn't all bad here. She hung around after surgery on Wednesday evening.

'Can we talk?' she asked. His heart

sinking, Madoc invited her to sit down in the kitchen over a coffee.

'You've decided to go, haven't you?'

'I'm afraid so.' She felt tears burning at the back of her eyes and swallowed them down.

'Is there nothing I can do or say to make you change your mind?' He reached for her hand over the table and she felt even worse. His touch was gentle and it nearly broke her heart when she shook her head.

'I'd like to go as soon as possible. Emma will be back next week and now the holidaymakers have mostly all gone, the patient load will lessen. You should be able to get a locum fairly easily at this time of year.'

'There's never be anyone better than you. I was going to offer you the partnership.'

'I know, but it's more than just the work.' She could control herself no longer and the tears came. 'I'm sorry, I must go now. Please contact the agency and find a replacement for me as soon as possible,' she sobbed as she ran out of the surgery.

Back in her cottage, she sat miserably drinking a mug of chocolate. She had guessed the partnership in the practice was going to be on offer, but it was the fact that she was falling in love with someone who was so unsuitable, that had clinched her decision. She would go and stay with her parents for a while until a job came up. She had saved a lot while she had been here with virtually no rental and with few things on which she might spend her money. It was a good job she hadn't followed her intention to buy a boat. She remembered the day they had gone sailing and the dramatic rescue. She had certainly gained plenty of experience since she had been here.

* * *

Dreading the following morning, Nick arrived slightly later than usual. To her surprise, Emma was sitting at her desk, looking fully in charge and very much better than when Nick had last visited her.

'Emma, how lovely to see you. But you're not due back till next week. Are you sure you should be here?'

'I'm feeling fine. The medicine you gave me has worked wonders. I've had no symptoms for days now and I was getting bored. Besides, I've been hearing dire tales of queues and missed appointment times. High time I was back here sorting you out.'

'That's really great but for goodness sake, don't overdo it. I hope you didn't walk up that hill this morning.'

'Of course not. Derek dropped me off on his way to work. And he's collecting me at the end of the day. We've both learned a lesson from all of this. Gentle exercise without any strain. That's my rule from now on. And no more clotted cream teas and pasties. Salads and fruit. Derek's already lost three pounds. Mind you, he hates it all and I'm sure he's sneaking off to the pasty shop some days. Now, here's your list for this morning so far and I'll have your house calls ready later.'

'Emma, you're a genius.' Somehow, all seemed to be calm and back to normal with everything running smoothly. Madoc had already left to take his morning clinic in the next village so she didn't even have to face him.

Nothing about her leaving was mentioned again during the week. She had broken the news to Emma on Friday afternoon but the receptionist seemed to know already.

'He asked me to type a letter to the agency so I guessed you'd decided to leave us. I'm really sorry. I had hoped you'd become a permanent fixture here. I suppose Madoc's anti-woman phobia became too much?'

'Not really. It's complicated. At least I know he's organising a replacement. I hope to go very soon.'

'We had a call from the agency this morning. They're sending someone for an interview on Monday.'

'Wow. Amazing. I wasn't expecting it to be quite so soon. Who is it?'

'Someone over from New Zealand. He's doing some sort of research and wanted a small practice to get experience for a couple of months. The thing is, he can start immediately.'

'Great,' Nick managed to squeal. She felt her heart thumping unnaturally and the top of her head was flying away into the distance. She could be leaving much sooner than she had ever dreamed of and now it was happening, everything and everywhere here seemed very dear to her. This was by far the best thing for both her and Madoc, she tried to reason. A quick clean break now the decision was made.

'Well, see you on Monday. Have a nice weekend.'

★ ★ ★

Madoc was still out somewhere so she had a couple of days to acclimatise to the huge changes that were impending.

She would need to clear out of the cottage quickly as this new man would need it. She would surely work the next week at least, if only to ensure a smooth hand over to her replacement. She looked around the little place and knew she was going to miss it terribly. And all the patients she had come to know and like. And the village and the gossipy folk she had been uncertain about. It was all her own choice, she told herself, her own decision. She could be gone by next weekend.

She needed to call her parents and break the news to them and make sure she could stay with them for a while. Tomorrow, she decided. Or Sunday. Not tonight. She decided that she would go and eat at the pub that evening and not mope around the house. She would only get herself into a miserable state and become even more maudlin.

'Hello, love,' said the landlord. 'On your own tonight? No Doctor Roskelly to keep you company?'

'Not tonight. I was too weary to cook

for myself so I thought I'd come for one of your amazing steaks. And a large glass of red wine please.'

'Coming up. There's a window table if you'd like it or a corner table if you prefer.'

'I'll go for the window please. Look over the harbour and enjoy the view.' She sat contemplating the first time they had sat here. Careful to avoid gossip, they had sat out openly for everyone to see. She sipped the wine and watched as one or two boats left the harbour for the night's fishing.

'Would it be all right if I joined you?' a voice said from behind her. She jumped and swung round.

'Madoc. What are you doing here?'

'I called to see you at the cottage but you weren't there. I saw your car still parked outside and made a guess where to find you. I was going to ask you to join me for dinner here.'

'First time, last time.'

'I see what you mean. I gather you've ordered?'

'I'm having a steak. Hope it won't bother you. Please, sit down if you'd like to.'

'Thank you. Of course I don't mind if you eat steak. As long as I don't have to.' The landlord arrived to take his order.

'Shall I hold yours back so you can eat together?'

'If you can manage it without it spoiling. Thanks.'

'I'll have a small glass of dry white wine and some soda water in it,' Madoc said, surprising all of them.

'Right sir. One spritzer coming up.'

'Goodness Madoc. That's alcoholic, you realise.'

'Times are changing around here. Thought I'd join in. I, er, gather that Emma spoke to you about the interview on Monday? I'd be grateful if you'd sit in on it. I'd like your opinion.'

'Really?' she muttered.

'Yes please. If he takes up the job, I'd like you to stay on at least for the week to make sure he's on the right lines.

He'll only be here for a short time anyway but I don't want too many problems. It's unfair to the patients.'

It seemed a rather difficult evening. Both of them had emotions running high and though eventually, the wine relaxed them, the underlying tensions were too much. The look in Madoc's eyes was almost too much for Nick to bear. He looked so sad and hurt and she wanted to hug him better. Despite his tough lion like exterior, she could see the man beneath who had been left so unhappy by his unsatisfactory marriage. He seemed very different to the man she had first met in the surgery all those months ago. They walked together up the hill.

'So, you can work with a woman after all,' she said, voicing her thoughts.

'Apparently so. But I can't manage to have a relationship with one. I suppose I'm too late to persuade you to change your mind, Nicola?' He caught her hand in his and tried to pull her close. She felt her heart race once more but she forced herself to pull away.

'Yes. You are too late. There are too many issues. Goodnight, Madoc. And thank you for the meal. I'd really rather have paid for myself though.' There had been a slight argument in the pub but she had given in, not wanting to cause a scene in public.

* * *

She scuttled into her cottage and shut the door quickly so he couldn't follow her or say anything else. It was all getting much too painful. She just had to get through the weekend and maybe this time next week, she would be driving back to her parents' home. She had to make the most of this, her final few days in this beautiful place. Tomorrow, she would explore the far West. Look at Lands End and some of the pretty places along the South Coast. She hadn't been there for many years. There would be plenty of time to pack up her belongings later in the week.

She set off early the next morning and drove to the far tip of England and the country. It was a slightly dull day but the light was clear. She could look out to sea and just see the bumps on the horizon that were the Scilly Isles. She would have enjoyed a day trip over there but there may not be time now.

She avoided the various tourist attractions and walked along the rugged cliffs, watching a pod of dolphins leaping from the water. Amazing creatures, she thought. There were seals basking on the rocks too and she wished she had brought her camera. It was unlike her to have forgotten it but her mind was still in some sort of turmoil. Madoc would have enjoyed this, she kept thinking. Pity she hadn't asked him to join her. Ironic really, as this time last week they were walking together nearer home.

Madoc. Madoc. Madoc. When would the man get out of her mind? Not until she left Cornwall far behind her. A black bird flew up in front of her. A large black bird with bright red legs and a red beak.

'Oh,' she gasped. 'It's a chough.' There were only a very few of the birds left and they were usually such a rare sight. They were the symbol of Cornwall and it seemed so significant to her on this, her last weekend in the county. I must tell Madoc, she thought. But then, he may not be interested. She went back to her car and drove back along the coast, stopping off at various places on her way.

Exhausted once more, she got back to her home as night was falling. On Sunday, she decided to spend the day sorting things out and doing several loads of washing. The little clothes line in the garden was filled a number of times and she also left things dripping over the bath. At least when she went home next week, it wouldn't be with the traditional loads of dirty washing for her mother to sort out.

She had still put off calling her parents and decided she might leave it till later in the week. In any case, this locum coming the next day might not be suitable. Perhaps she was beginning to hope not, despite all her decision making.

★ ★ ★

While she was taking her surgery the next morning, Nick heard the outer door open and Emma greeting someone who was not one of the usual patients. She saw her last patient out and saw a good looking, youngish man sitting on one of the seats. Emma rose as Nick put the patient records down on her desk.

'Nick, this is Justin. He's from New Zealand and here for an interview.' Emma was positively gushing. He stood up, a gangly young man who scarcely looked old enough to be qualified. He held out a hand.

'G'd day,' he said loudly. 'Good to meet you.' The accent was strong and not quite the familiar Australian twang but very similar.

'Hello. I'm Nick. It's my job you're here for.'

'You going then? Mind if I ask why?'

'Complicated. But, there's nothing wrong with the practice, I assure you. Just time for me to move on I suppose. It was always a temporary appointment anyhow.'

'Oh, OK. So what's the set-up? The agency was a bit sketchy. I was just delighted to get an interview so quickly. I only arrived here last week so couldn't believe my luck when I made it here. What's the surfing like?' Nick gave a smile. Not one of Madoc's priorities there.

'Some good beaches around. Can be good down here but usually better on one of the bigger bays.'

'Sweet. You a surfer chick then?' Nick grinned.

'Not exactly a chick any more but yes, I do go out occasionally. Now, if you'll excuse me for a few minutes, I need to tidy up after my surgery.'

She wasn't quite sure what Madoc would make of this one. She tidied her desk and straightened her drawer. Anything to delay going out there again and having to make small talk to the person who could be about to replace her. She heard Madoc go out and introductions being made. When she felt it safe to join them, she left her room and went into the reception area. The outer door was locked and Emma settled down at her desk to sort her own work.

Madoc invited them to go into his room and the interview began. Justin sounded a bit more professional when he spoke to Madoc and Nick felt herself a little superficial to the proceedings.

'You do realise this is a very temporary position?' Madoc said after about half an hour of questioning.

'Sure thing. That's what I was looking for. Experience of a small rural practice. I'm researching various set-ups in the UK and there's nothing like working there to see what they're really like. I appreciate the chance you're offering.'

'Well, I haven't exactly offered yet. But I suppose we can work together for a couple of months, unless I get an applicant for the permanent position in the meantime. If that's good for you, let's start with a couple of weeks' trial.'

'Excellent,' Justin said. 'When do I start?'

'Soon as you can.'

'Got my kit in the hire car. Just need to find somewhere to stay and I'm good to go.'

They sorted out a few details and Madoc shook the young man's hand.

'Welcome aboard. Nicola will show you the routine and I suggest you shadow her for a day or two. OK with you Nicola?'

'I suppose so. I'll be moving out of my cottage at the end of the week so maybe you'll be able to take that over? The pub's very good and they have rooms at this time of year.'

'Probably easier if you stay here at

my place,' Madoc offered. Nick almost hated him for being so welcoming, but realised she had no right to feel that way. How different from her own initial greeting here.

'I must get on with my rounds,' she said. 'You could come out with me tomorrow if you want to get a feel for the area.'

She left, feeling his appointment might have been a little hasty. But, it was not her problem. When she came back, Emma was looking distinctly harassed.

'What is it Emma?' she asked anxiously. 'Are you feeling unwell?'

'Not at all. It's this new chap Madoc's set on taking on. Never stops asking questions and wanting things. Seems to have taken over your office already. Do you really have to go? I thought you were getting on so well. Please, Nick, won't you re-consider and stay on?'

'I can't, Emma. Anyway, it's too late now. Justin's been offered the job. Only temporary but it's still an offer.'

'This is going to be a disaster. And I'm really going to miss you. We all are. The patients are very fond of you and especially some of the young mums with babies. They feel they can really communicate with you. And I thought you and Madoc, well . . . there might be a little spark there? He's been so much more cheerful lately.'

'Sorry, Emma. I just have to move on.'

'Well, I'm sorry too. Really sorry. Thought you seemed so happy. But, who can tell what's going on inside? So, when are you going?'

'Friday, all being well. I'm going to stay with my parents for a while and then look for somewhere permanent. Time to put down roots, as I keep saying.'

'We'll have to have a little send off then after work on Friday.'

Nick protested that there was no need but had to give in. It would be a chance to say goodbye and thanks to those who had supported her. She really should call on Auntie Dolly and make sure she knew she was leaving. Maybe she should have given notice but it was too late now. If she wanted rent in lieu of notice, that would be fine. She'd scarcely paid anything for the rent anyway.

'Come in, dear,' Auntie Dolly called, without asking who was there.

'Only me.'

'Yes Nick, I know. Come to give me notice have you?'

'I'm afraid so. Rather short notice too.'

'Shame. Still, it's not too late for you and my boy to get together. Will you do something for me?'

'Of course. What is it? Shopping to collect or something?'

'Course not. No, I want you to stay on for a week. Have yourself a little holiday. I'm not letting that young man have my cottage. Don't know what he might get up to. He can stay with my boy until he packs it in. He won't last long, mark my words. So, what do you say? You'll stay in the cottage for one more week? There's places you haven't seen around here. I think you'll be going out on the sea one more time.'

Nick gave a start. Scilly Isles flashed into her mind. If she stayed on for a holiday, she could spend a day over there. It was tempting.

'OK, thank you. I will stay for a holiday. But I shall insist on paying proper rent. You must have lost out on a whole summer's rents coming in.'

'Nonsense. I've got all I need. It's been nice to know it's been looked after and I haven't had to pay for someone to go in and clean after holiday makers. Now you and my boy will come for supper. Thursday evening. Six o'clock.'

'Thank you. That's kind. But there's Justin to consider.'

'He'll look after himself. It'll all work out for you, mark my words. You just have to do as you're told for once.'

Nick laughed to herself as she went back to Myrtle Cottage. It was fortunate she hadn't got round to telling her parents about the changes. She must have her own version of sixth sense.

The rest of the week was exhausting. Justin asked questions all the time, both to her and the patients. The visits were taking longer each day and she seemed to be in a constant rush to catch up. She tried telling him to ask less but he simply grinned and said that research meant asking lots of questions. Emma was thoroughly fed up with him and Madoc seemed to be feeling a bit of a strain having to share his home with the young man. Nor was he too pleased when she told him that Auntie Dolly had all but insisted she stay on for an extra week for a holiday.

'I was hoping he'd move out at the weekend,' he said. 'Oh and by the way, are you all right with this supper party thing Auntie Dolly's organising?'

'I suppose so. I was a bit concerned that she wasn't inviting Justin.'

'Don't worry about him. He's already

checking out the local talent. Got his eye on a couple of girls in the village. What do you think of him?'

'I'm not sure. He talks a lot. Asks a lot of questions but I can't say I've heard much in the way of diagnosis or treatment.'

'I agree. Still, he may be the best I can hope for in the circumstances. I suppose you haven't had second thoughts?' She shook her head as she walked away. Each day seemed more painful and produced more things she was going to miss. She couldn't trust herself not to give in.

★ ★ ★

All too soon, it was Thursday evening and they met on the doorstep at Auntie Dolly's cottage.

'Come in my dears,' she chortled. 'Handsome pair you do make.'

'Now Auntie Dolly, don't say things like that or Nicola here will up and off before she's even tasted your fish pie.'

'How do you know that's what you're getting?'

'You're not the only one with special powers you know. Runs in the family.' Nick laughed. They were so funny together and she always saw a different side to Madoc when he was with his aunt. They were clearly very close.

'So, whose sister are you?' she asked. 'Madoc's mother or father?'

'His granddad, if you must know. That surprise you? I'm older than I look, obviously.' She gave one of her cackles. Now, sit you down. I've got a nice glass of wine for you. Homemade it is and non-alcoholic of course.' She poured a clear amber coloured liquid into the three glasses and handed them round. 'Here you are. Now drink up.'

It was delicious, though Nick would have questioned the non-alcoholic label that she gave with it. She felt a warm glow as it went down and complimented the old lady.

'That is gorgeous. You could sell that

by the bucket load if it really is non-alcoholic. What's in it?'

'Never ask Auntie Dolly such questions. You might not want to know. Eye of toad and wing of bat and all that. But it's usually harmless.'

'Course it is. Besides, it wouldn't be vegetarian if it had all those things in. I'm not that sort of witch you know. Only use herbs and natural things you find in the hedgerows.'

'All the same,' Madoc continued, 'best not to know.' Auntie Dolly looked pleased by his comments.

'Now then, sit you down. Side by side, that's it.' She went into her little kitchen.

'Ever felt we were being pushed together?' Nick whispered.

'This is what she's all about. I did try to talk to her yesterday and tried to stop her pushing us but it was no good. I'm sorry.' Nick smiled resignedly as Auntie Dolly came in with a large fish pie. 'Wow, that looks well up to your usual standard,' he said.

'Looks fabulous. Thank you. Smells wonderful too. I've just realised how hungry I am.'

It was a pleasant evening. The non-alcoholic wine had certainly relaxed them all and Nick felt better than she had for several days. By the time the meal was over, she felt very full and rather sleepy.

'Off you go now, you two,' Auntie Dolly said when it was barely nine o'clock. 'When you get to my age, you need your sleep.'

'Can't we at least help with the washing up?' Nick offered.

'Certainly not. I shall merely wave my magic wand and it will all be done in no time.'

'She actually means she will load the dishwasher,' Madoc informed her.

'Don't you go ruining my reputation young man. Sweet dreams to you. Clear off now.'

Laughing, they walked up the hill together.

'She's such a case,' Nick said. 'She

does look like a witch though doesn't she?'

'She tries. Scares all the little kids with her threats of magic and such. But she does know a great deal about herbs and their properties. She has occasionally been able to cure things that conventional medicines can't manage.'

'Well, here I am. Back home again. Home for a little longer.'

'You all right with this gathering Emma's organising? There will be one or two patients who specially asked to be there and Alice Penweather, the midwife. I should also warn you, there's been a collection and a presentation will follow.'

'Oh no. How embarrassing. I really don't deserve it. I've only been doing my job.'

'Well, it's happened and I thought you might prefer to know in advance. Well, goodnight my dear.' He gave her a peck on the cheek and then hesitated as if he wanted to say or do something more. Instead, he turned and walked quickly away.

$$\star \quad \star \quad \star$$

All too soon, it was Friday evening. Emma had been busy all afternoon, sending Nick home as soon as she had finished her surgery. As she sat in her lounge, she could see various people passing up and down the hill, carrying tins and plastic boxes. The van from the village stores also went up the hill. Nick was beginning to feel nervous about the coming event.

She hated being the centre of attention and in any case, she had only been there for a relatively short time. It was all too much. She went to change out of her working clothes, thinking she'd better made a bit of an effort if all these folks were doing the same.

At the appointed time, she made her way to the surgery for what was probably her last visit. She had already cleared her desk, packing away the

Pooh Bear clock and wondering where it might be finding its next home. There was already quite a crowd in the reception area when she arrived.

'Goodness,' she said nervously. 'How kind of you all to come here.' She was handed a glass of wine and she wandered round, trying to make sure she spoke to everyone. Justin was already downing his second can of beer and chatting loudly to anyone who'd listen or not be listening. Madoc was standing looking uncomfortably formal in a suit and tie. He announced supper was ready and everyone turned to the heavily laden table. It seemed that most of the village had contributed pies and cakes, savouries and tiny pasties. It was a wonderful spread.

When everyone had eaten, Madoc called for silence.

'As you all know, we're here tonight to say goodbye to the best locum I could ever have hoped to find. I know she has made a great hit with you all and despite my doubts about her when she arrived, I consider it a privilege to have known and worked with Nicola Quenby. Nick as she likes to be called. Raise your glasses to Nick please, ladies and gentlemen.'

'To Nick,' they chorused.

'And please accept this gift as a token of our appreciation. Take care. It's fragile.' Madoc handed her a large square box which was rather heavy. 'Speech', was called by everyone. Blushing furiously, Nick began.

'I'm quite overwhelmed by all of this. Firstly, I must thank Emma for organising this evening. And all of you who have contributed to such a magnificent spread. And to everyone who has contributed to this present. I can't wait to open it. And mostly, thanks to Madoc for being such a wonderfully caring doctor. You're lucky to have him and I've been lucky to work with him for the past months. Can I open my present now?' she finished with a giggle.

They all clapped and cheered. She

lifted the lid off the box and saw a beautiful locally made dish. It was a large piece of studio pottery, decorated in sea colours and something she would always cherish. 'It's just fabulous. Thank you all so much.'

'I hope you really like it,' Emma said anxiously. 'Only I wanted to get something you would associate with Cornwall and your time with us.'

'It's lovely. Really lovely and I couldn't be more delighted with it. Thank you again. I just hope you haven't overdone things today.'

'Not at all. And it's good news from the consultant. I don't have to have any further investigation. They are keeping me on various pills and no operation.'

'That's really good news. A warning shot though.' She gave Emma a hug and felt tears once more pricking her eyes. She glanced at Justin. He was definitely the worse for wear and reeling against the door in a most unprofessional way. She hoped he wasn't going to prove a total disaster.

It took an hour more before everyone had left. Not wanting to go back to her cottage alone, Nick stayed to help clear up. Justin went to his room, presumably to put himself to bed to get over his excesses. Finally, Madoc and Nick were left alone.

'I can't tell you how sorry I am that you are going.'

'I'm staying for the rest of the week. Auntie Dolly insisted I have a bit of a holiday. I'd like to go over to the Scilly Isles for a day and do a bit of touring around. Make the most of my time here.'

'I suppose you wouldn't like some company? We could go over on the helicopter, maybe tomorrow?' Nick hesitated.

'Well, if you're sure. That would be good. Much more fun than going alone, assuming we can get seats of course.'

'I'll go on-line right away. See what I can do.' Five minutes later he returned. 'Tresco all right with you? We have to be at the heliport by nine.'

281

'Excellent. Wonderful in fact.'

It was a beautiful day as they walked around the tiny island, stopping at the hotel for a delightful meal. It was an island where you never lost touch with the sea nor could you forget it was an island. There were still plenty of wild flowers and to her delight, Nick saw her first puffin. She was so thrilled. Madoc smiled at her and even dared to take her hand as they walked back towards the Abbey Gardens.

'This is a truly magical place,' she whispered as they wandered among the exotic plants and shrubs. 'Just look at those trees. Amazing.'

All too soon, it was time to return to catch their helicopter back to the mainland.

'I feel as if I've been in another world entirely,' she said. 'It's so relaxing and peaceful.'

'No traffic, I suspect,' Madoc replied. 'But I agree. It's been like a real holiday.'

They flew back and she gazed out of the window.

'There's the ferry, look Madoc. It's like a toy boat. Oh and are those basking sharks? Look.' The pilot announced that he had spotted basking sharks below and everyone else peered down to see the huge harmless creatures. Nick smiled. 'I saw them first.'

They flew low over Lands End and then along the South coast where she had driven the previous weekend. Penzance came into view and long before she was ready, they were landing at the heliport.

'What a perfect day,' she said as they drove back to Gwillian.

'You know, there could be plenty more of them, if you stayed.'

'I know. Madoc, you do know I have feelings for you?'

'I had hoped so. But I still don't understand why you want to leave if you care.'

'It's . . . well, the main thing is your attitude to children. I've always wanted to have children and could never imagine a life without them.'

'And I could never imagine a life with them. I'm scared Nicola. Scared that we could be close and that you'd be bored with me, just as my ex-wife became bored. She wanted children because she thought it might make her happy. I didn't think that could possibly work.'

'I agree. You need to be friends first and foremost. We're friends, aren't we? Then love can grow. From that love, one becomes complete with the children.' She paused. If they were to admit that they had fallen in love, could that ultimately be enough? If they didn't have children, could she be happy and fulfilled? It was possible with a man like Madoc. She drew breath to say the words.

'Hush, Nicola,' he said. He stopped the car in a layby, leaned over to kiss her gently on the lips. 'If I asked you to marry me and I agreed that we should try to have children, what would you say?'

The colour rose in her cheeks.

'If you asked me to marry you, I might have to say yes. If you said you'd simply consider having a family, I'd have to shout yes, very loudly. If you asked of course.'

'I can't bear to think of you going from my life. If I have to compromise, then it has to be. I think I'd agree to anything to keep you here. My dearest Nicola. I never dreamed I would say this to another woman, but I do truly love you. I hadn't realised it until I thought I was losing you.'

He had said everything she had wanted to hear. She could stay in this place with a man she knew she loved and who loved her back. She could keep the job she loved and live in a community she had grown to respect.

'What really changed your mind?' she asked when they were back at her cottage.

'That witch I call my Auntie. She gave me a talking to last night after the party. Made me realise that I shouldn't make conditions. That true love is something to be cherished. I hadn't even been certain that the confusion of feelings that have been tormenting me were indeed, true love.'

'I hadn't realised you'd been to see her. She clearly does speak some good sense at times. Did you have anything to drink at her place?'

'Just some of her homemade, non-alcoholic wine. The stuff we had the other day.'

'I wonder,' Nick mused. 'Never mind.'

'You think she fed me one of her dratted love potions?'

'Maybe she fed it to both of us. She claims they are very reliable and last forever.'

'Bet she'll never admit it.'

'You realise we have a couple of problems now? I've been given a leaving present, something they made a collection to provide.'

'It will have to be a wedding present, won't it? And the other problem?'

'Justin. You've given him a contract

for a couple of weeks.'

'Excellent. It means we can spend time planning the wedding. I'd prefer a small affair with just close family. What do you think?'

'I'd never have believed that any of this could happen in so short a time, my handsome lion.'

'I'm just a pussycat really.'

'So I've been told.'

They kissed and Nick knew she had finally come home to where she wanted to be for the rest of her life.

THE END

We do hope that you have enjoyed reading this large print book.

Did you know that all of our titles are available for purchase?

We publish a wide range of high quality large print books including:
Romances, Mysteries, Classics
General Fiction
Non Fiction and Westerns

Special interest titles available in large print are:
The Little Oxford Dictionary
Music Book, Song Book
Hymn Book, Service Book

Also available from us courtesy of Oxford University Press:
Young Readers' Dictionary
(large print edition)
Young Readers' Thesaurus
(large print edition)

For further information or a free brochure, please contact us at:
Ulverscroft Large Print Books Ltd.,
The Green, Bradgate Road, Anstey,
Leicester, LE7 7FU, England.
Tel: (00 44) **0116 236 4325**
Fax: (00 44) **0116 234 0205**

Other titles in the
Linford Romance Library:

CYPRUS DREAM

Sheila Holroyd

Lorna had come to Cyprus reluctantly, as her aunt's holiday companion. There she met James, who helped her to find out that there was more to the island than hotels and beaches. But could he save her when a ruthless scheme to exploit the island's beauty put her in deadly danger? What would happen to their growing friendship when the holiday was over? And what were her aunt's secret plans?

CHATEAU OF THE NYMPH

Sheila Daglish

When Jenna goes to work in her aunt's French hotel, she finds that someone is determined to force her family out. Is it the darkly forbidding Luc de Villiers? Centuries ago, the son of the lord of the chateau had fallen in love with the girl from the village inn. Was history repeating itself? Only when Jenna's life is put in danger does she discover the truth behind the chateau's legend and find love in place of long-ago tragedy.